Paper, Scissors, Rock

Paper, Scissors, Rock

Ann Decter

PRESS GANG PUBLISHERS
VANCOUVER

The Publisher gratefully acknowledges financial assistance from the Canada Council.

Canadian Cataloguing in Publication Data

   Decter, Ann, 1956–
      Paper, scissors, rock

      ISBN 0-88974-040-2

      I. Title.
   PS8557.E27P3   1992   C813'.54   C92-091581-7
   PR9199.3.D32P3   1992

First Printing September 1992
         2   3   4   5   96   95   94   93

Edited by Barbara Kuhne and Robin Van Heck
Cover and text design by Valerie Speidel
Cover art by Janice Wong, *The Space Between* 1990 (Detail), Oil on canvas, 3' x 4'.
   Collection of the artist.
Author photograph by Rachel Epstein
Typeset in Meridien at The Typeworks
Printed on acid-free paper by Best Gagné Book Manufacturers Inc.
Printed and bound in Canada

Press Gang Publishers
603 Powell Street
Vancouver, B.C.   V6A 1H2
Canada

For West Hawk, and everyone who shared it.

ACKNOWLEDGEMENTS

Heartfelt thank-yous to Allan Decter for sharing history, to Wendy Waring for reading and seeing, to John, Michael, Richard, Loreto and Hana for books and research assistance, to Derry, Becky, Irene, Leah, Angela, Lois and Lillian for encouragement and support, and to Maureen for listening and comfort. Many thanks to the women of Press Gang Publishers for their skills and enthusiasm in making this book.

You have to go home again, in some way or other.

MARGARET LAURENCE
The Diviners

I

HATRED

Perhaps in these same pines runs,
with cross ties of bleeding thorns,
the track of the Underground Rail-
road way up into Canada,
and what links the Appalachians
is the tinkle of ankle chains
running north, where history is harder
to bear: the hypocrisy
of clouds with Puritan collars.

DEREK WALCOTT
The Arkansas Testament

Memory is a stone.

Snip.
Clippers snip bush undergrowth overgrowth over still rock. Mute granite
same size shape texture gazes up indifferent, unchanged as dense years
wove a rampant weed cloak. Rampant years, dense cloak.
Gazes through a hole in time.

Sew to heel. Heal to sow.
Head to toe. Or is it toe to head?

Head to toe Jane is no taller than she was as a teenager. Her body is
smaller, weaker, less agile, more thoughtful. Her skin knows men, and
women. Touching and touched. Chooses. She is aware of false dichoto-
mies, treacherous language, logical terror; of log jams and pile-ups, plane
crashes and genocide for profit. She longs for a philosophy of emotion,
an ethic of reason, an economic system motivated by conscience, for pre-
history, post-history, and a loose thread with which to unravel, slowly
and carefully, a whole pattern. Warp and weft. Consciously bereft. And
so snips.
Toe to head Jane is not at all who she was as a teenager. Confidence rises
and falls, accidents are expected, acts have consequences that demand to
be assessed before action is taken. Wait and witness. Her hearing is
multi-layered, requiring all of Jane's being. To speak is to venture into
the world, Jane taking a chance on arriving. Vulnerability, possibility.
And so she chooses carefully what she snips. With an awareness of
growth, and space, with a knowledge that shielding pain and fear is not
protection. Chooses.
Toe to head.

The land Jane is clearing is Canadian shield, pre-Cambrian, lava cooled and hardened over 2,000 million years. The bush she snips, introduced to the shield sixty years ago to provide a simple hedge around the cabin, is called caragana. Untended for ten years, it shrouds the world below its six feet, a landscape of thin soil, fungus, mosses and lichens that grow on the stone of the aging shield. Only old pines are visible above the shroud. It is bush her mother cut and taught her to cut, the years before these past ten. She cuts where her mother would have, would have wanted her to, would have known what had to be cut away. Sophia. Knew, and taught Jane. Cut it back or it will choke other life.

There is so much more cutting to be done, now, after all the neglect. Sophia has been gone a long time. And more than once. Wild berries no longer grow here. No buttercups, rosehips, blue bells, or wild orchids, no long grass going gently to seed. Hazelnuts, birch, poplar and spruce are stunted by the green shroud. Mosquitoes cluster and breed in its cool damp shade. Jane eyes a pine, cuts toward it, clipping through stems at knee level. Snip, snip, snip snip snip. Bushes, already grown to trees, fall away from their narrow trunks into her hands. The shroud opens above her. Sunlight soothes rust pine needles at her feet. Jane pulls off a tattered glove, brushes needles away and lays her hand on a rock. Still cool, even as work and sun warm her. Still.

Jane sees a birch struggling two yards away, leaves suffused in a thrall of caragana.
"I'm coming," she announces and cuts toward it. Feels the foreign weed laughing at her, mocking her as she mocked crows the day before, answering caw for caw, certain they didn't know they were speaking to a woman. Caragana laughs soundlessly, winding its reckless imported branches around the birch, bursting its pea pods in the afternoon heat. A soft crackle. Seeds nestle and sow, to sprout again. And strangle. Strangle hold.
Snip, snip, snip snip snip snip

A rock is a stone.
Jane's hand on a hole in time.
Years ago, mother and daughter came home from a party. Years ago. A family party, rites of passage. They sat in the car, talking. Sophia and Jane.
"He tried to strangle me once," Sophia said, turning off the motor. She

spoke as the woman he had tried to strangle. She got out of the car. He. HusbandfatherPhil.

"Don't tell me." Jane's stomach curled. "I don't want to hear this." She hurried out the other side, slamming the door after herself.

"Well, he did," her mother answered flatly, walking away.

"Stop. Stop it. Please—stop." Jane followed. Fear crept behind, up the stairs and into the bedroom. Jane slumped on his side of the bed. Sophia lay beside her, face down on the richly textured bedspread. Golds and browns, deep green and rust. Forest colours. Sophia chose them consistently.

"I'll be stuck here," Sophia spit the words. "He'll be in a wheelchair and I'll be stuck here taking care of him for years and years. Just like Baba and Zeda . . . the bastard!"

"Stop, stop it—just go. Go, please." Jane whined, arms tightening stomach tightening mind tightening.

"I'll end up his nurse," Sophia moaned, breathing in the stale stench of sacrifice and dreams denied.

"So-phia! Stop."

Jane tried to staunch the flow, unable to grasp that Sophia no longer cared about a man who faced a lingering death. Wanted her freedom more. Did not care, she who had taught Jane caring. Spat venom to coil inside Jane. Inside the coil, Jane sought the pattern of her love for Sophia. "Just—uh—go," she grunted. The pattern of support and permission and belief in Sophia's dreams and desires as separate from Phil's.

Sophia lifted her head. Eyes wild and furious. "How?" Brittle.

Jane began to cry, to weep, for herself. Sophia could not be placated. Sophia, too, became dangerous. The safe parent who had protected her children from the viciousness of Phil's moods. "I—can't—stand—this." Jane forced herself to speak, meant to scream, and never knew if she had. The words were far away, drifting, like Sophia. Far away.

Jane's older brother, Owen, finally interrupted them, still crying and arguing on the parents' bed. Separated them, for Jane could neither succumb to the bitterness nor ignore it and go to bed. Ignoring Sophia's unhappiness was not part of the pattern. Owen was irritated with them for squabbling while Phil, their father and husband, was in hospital for tests. What could they be thinking of?

He wanted, instead, a moment to tell them Phil was alright, everything was alright.

As alright as it could be.

Phil's tests were ok. The next day, he was home.

Jane was nineteen.

Stone.

A rock, cliff, crag, rocky ground or mass of rock. Rocky mountains. Massive rock. An emblem of motionlessness, fixity, harshness, insensibility. Soft now, beneath Jane's hand. Smooth and rough, mossy in part, warming so slowly as sun finally reaches it. Imperceptibly.

Jane looks at the stubs of the caragana she has cut. Open wood wounds. Stands and feels the space around her, the breeze beginning to ease through the few yards she has cleared. Through her, fresh and clear. Caragana will sprout again before June is over, small branches, low to the ground. But there will still be six feet above it, six feet that has not been here for years. Like Jane.

Memory. The faculty by which things are remembered. People, events, names, places dates emotions smells insipid song lyrics on pop radio that jolt you back decades so quickly you can't hate them anymore. Because they move you to a place you haven't been for so long.
Maybe that's what maturing really is. Losing the capacity to hate so quickly and vehemently. Physically, easily, a gut reaction. Maybe that's why some people look so young.
Children.
"I hate you"
"I hate you too"
"I hated you first"
"You can't come to my birthday party."
Clean shots, direct hits. No tangled knots of would haves and should haves and maybe she didn't really mean it and he might not be feeling too well and something else is really the problem, he's just taking it out on me. He's just. Block.
For the sake of the kids.
Minutes later kids' hate is forgotten, they're playing together again. That, too, gets lost. The dissipation. Easy come, easy go.
Sweet home Chi-ca-go.

Hatred, though, is a different kettle of fish.
Why malign fish?
A completely different knowledge.
In your nervous system.

Chicago is a city Jane has never visited.

"Though your brother's bound and gagged and they've chained him to a chair ... " as Jane turns it on, the old radio in the cabin evokes a Chicago of her mind. Jane lays the clippers down, takes off the cotton gloves through which tiny thorns have pierced her fingers. Slips off twenty years.

Memory's Chicago is the Democratic national convention, 1968. Is Mayor Richard Daley and the most reliable political machine in the United States. Is mace and truncheons and paramilitary police. All of which Jane heard on this old radio. Read about it in newspapers and magazines, listened as her parents discussed it.
Mace and truncheons and a British Labour MP, sprayed with mace by the Chicago police. A large woman; in Jane's memory she wore black, though why would she, here, in summer?
Jane knows the woman wore sunglasses to hide her swollen face, the blisters on her cheeks and eyelids that Jane did not see. Only the swelling was visible, puffy pink skin on which the glasses rested, as if they were too small for her. Her husband was smaller, also an MP. Jane remembers him as kind. For years after, they sent a card at Christmas.
They seemed like people Sophia would have known if she hadn't married Phil and come to Canada. It was like Sophia to be able to know them anyway. To bring them to her retreat, an old cabin in the Canadian bush, where they would talk about spending twenty-four hours in an American jail, about her face burning, about trying to convince the Chicago police that she was a member of the British House of Commons. And would they please call the British consulate and confirm? Did they? They must have, at some point.
"Won't you please come to Chicago?" the radio sings.

Phil had always liked receiving those cards. It made him proud. A Christmas card from two British MPs. The cards kept coming, even after she died, but with only his signature.

Chicago. One weekend in the late sixties a major freeway was closed. White people—European Americans—returning from cottages, were rerouted through a Black people's—African-American—neighbourhood. Their cars were stoned as they drove through. Jane listened to this news on the radio at her parents' cabin. People like Jane.

Later, Jane visited one Chicago by reading Richard Wright, when she was working with teenagers in downtown Toronto, a neighbourhood of Black, Portuguese and Chinese people. One of those summers when she did not come home to Muddy Water and the meteorite lake one hundred flat miles east of it.

Instead, she learned another face of racism, festering between cement and humidity.

As Jane saw it where she grew up, racism was what white people did to Métis and Cree, to Sioux and Ojibwa. How Anglophones and Anglo-philes did it to Francophones and Ukrainians and Jews. Had done it, to Phil. Until he beat the system that used to beat him. Earned his way out, but not quite in.

Paved his children's way in.

In the humid summer of downtown Toronto Jane had begun to learn about Black Canadian history, about communities founded and built by the freedom riders of the Underground Railway, communities a hundred years old and more. Older than the muddy prairie city where she grew up, older than the governments of the prairie provinces. Sophia, Jane's mother, immigrated to Canada, pregnant on a rolling ocean liner. So did Baba and Zeda, Phil's parents, exile children of the Pale. Europeans. A toe on this soil.

At the community centre, Jane learned about funk music and the real status of having gold jewellery possessing enough to loan it to friends. Learned ethnocentricity, one day when Jackie borrowed her demin jacket to go out in the rain. "Look like a white boy," he said, embarrassed to be wearing a second-hand jean jacket bought in Kensington market. Learned to say tape box, not "ghetto blaster." The limits of a culture. Hers.

Learned that the police would take two eight-year-old boys to the station because one of them hit a ten-year-old girl in the library. Because the librarian would phone the police, instead of phoning the boys' homes. Jane arrived at the library, with Jackie, in time to see the police car pulling away with his brother's and his nephew's little heads just visible above the car door. Wire mesh between them and the cops. Two Black boys.

Toronto, 1980.

Learned that as a person with white skin she might have lived in ignorance of the toll exacted by racism's weapons. Ashkenazi Jews passed now. Jewish and Irish, with no religion, she was perceived as Anglo-Canadian.

Mangia cake, the Portuguese kids said.

"But what does it mean?" Jane asked.

"Did your parents speak English at home?"

"Yes."

"So—you're a mangia cake."

While mangia cake Jane reflected on the privilege racism created, its choking motion wafted around her. Jackie tried to explain it to her once. Said, "When some ignorant white guy calls me a nigger, I can't see straight. My head just gets bigger and bigger and bigger, 'til I can't see straight. I don't even know what I'm doing."

Sweet home To-ron-to.

Sophia had taught her children never to say "nigger." And Jane could not say it. She felt nauseous when she first heard Lenny Bruce's skit on a record, where he said, "Nigger nigger nigger nigger nigger nigger nigger nigger nigger." Trying, like a child does, to say the word until it loses its meaning. Its power. To shock it out.

But language is social. You can't chant the meaning out of a word with so much history. Not by yourself.

"We're not allowed to say that word," Jane had explained to other kids, "we call this game 'Water Babies.'" She was embarrassed that Sophia might overhear the other kids saying it.

Jane didn't perceive any difference between saying it and saying it to somebody.

Sophia said Paul Robeson had once stayed in their house, before they bought it. The husband of the woman who sold it to Phil had been a concert promoter, and brought Paul Robeson to the city to perform. He could sing in Muddy Water, but he couldn't stay in a hotel there, because he was a Black genius.

Muddy water and it moves so slow. Thicker than blood.

Sophia always knew those kinds of things.

Canadian history is so different from American history. Ask Leonard Peltier.

Sophia played Paul Robeson records and wept. The spirituals. Played a tape of Dr. Martin Luther King, Jr.'s "I Have A Dream" speech over and over. Wept every time. Before he was murdered. Sophia knew the difference between crying and weeping. Later, much later, she wept when she heard Rita MacNeil and the Men Of The Deeps sing, "It's a workin' man I am, and I've been down underground, and I swear to God if I ever see the sun."

Though she never did swear to god.

At, maybe.

Sophia said the RCMP used to keep a list of unmarried men over thirty-two. Suspected homosexuals. Phil was thirty-three when he and Sophia got married. Svend Robinson was thirty-seven when he became the first Canadian Member of Parliament to publicly declare his homosexuality.

On February 29, 1988.

Later Jane wondered if that list wouldn't have been pretty long. And much later, after AIDS opened the closet door on so many, Jane tried to conjure a list of famous men who would have been on the list if the RCMP were still keeping it. That was before the evidence about ludicrous schemes for detecting homosexuals, the evidence of extortion and firings in the civil service under the watchful eyes of prime ministers for so many years, was released.

Death threat. Post mortem.

We are always with you. Even when you can't see us.

In sweet home Toronto, Jane learned about pawn shops, one day at the community centre when Gloria announced, gloating, "We're having a party at my house tomorrow. We always have really big parties." She was the youngest in a family of ten. "Before the party, my folks take all the gold out of the house, take it down to the pawn shop. That way," she wagged a wise finger at Jane, "they don't worry about it, no matter how big the party gets. It's just 'til the next day."

Jane came home that night to her walk-up apartment and told Shulamit, her roommate, Gloria's story. Shula promptly pawned all the gold items she owned. Israeli commemorative coins, a Star of David pendant, along with the pearl necklace from her grandfather who had bought and sold jewellery in Golder's Green after leaving France in advance of the German army invasion.

Shula was named after a grandmother, her Baba, who died in a concentration camp organized by Nazis.

"I think I'm anti-Semitic," Shula said one day.

"Why?" asked Jane.

"Because I hate Jews."

Pawning those things seemed to give Shulamit a sense of relief. "I can always get them back," Shula told her mother on the telephone.

Shulamit, they gave her death.

And you, you got her life.

Namesake. Keepsake.

Can't forsake.

Later, Jane learned of a group called Jewish Lesbian Daughters of the Holocaust.

Let freedom ring, Shula.

On Bathurst Street, Jane read Richard Wright, sat nervously with Jackie in McDonald's while Maria—his girlfriend—had an abortion on a school day, invited speakers from the Ban the Klan group, persuaded Maria to go on the pill after a second pregnancy scare, and screened movies from the library.

"Weren't white people ever slaves?" Jackie asked after watching *The Autobiography of Miss Jane Pittman.*

"Yes."

The movie the teenagers asked to see was a documentary about a program for juvenile offenders run by prisoners in maximumsecurity institutions. The drop-in quieted as a shot of teenagers, sitting in a circle, appeared on the screen. The camera shifted quickly to the harsh faces of the imprisoned men. Big men, hollering and swearing, hounding the youths with their knowledge of prison life.

"Think you can fuckin' take that? Think you can? Think you're a big man? In here you're nobody, no fuckin' body. Unnerstan'?"

"   "

"I said, unnerstan'?"

"Ye-ah." Whispered.

In the dark quiet room the teens watched intently. Rivetted.

When the movie ended, they were uncharacteristically calm. Then someone said it must be the American version. Denny, one of Susie's brothers, was rumoured to be in the Canadian version of the film. Seventeen, just out of jail. He hit a teacher on the head with a piece of wood when he was seven, and the teacher died. He spent a decade in jail.

He's hard, that Denny, the kids said.

He came around the drop-in once, a mask of stone on his finely featured face.

A Chicago of the mind.

That September, Jane's job ended. The community centre didn't want to go on funding a program for teenagers. Too much trouble. Jane thought she might go home to spend some time with Phil, before getting another job. More than five years had passed since the argument with Sophia that Jane did not remember, four since both mother and daughter had left Muddy Water. Years in which Jane had simply stayed away. The lapse of time had given Jane a sense that she had changed significantly and a desire to show Phil who she had become. A desire to see him for her own sake, for him to see her.

For her own sake.

Before it was too late.

Over a year later, Jane met Jackie on a street in Toronto. She was happy to see him after a year with Phil in Muddy Water.

"Hey, Jackie, hi, how are you?" Jane smiled. Good-looking kid, Jackie. Lots of spirit.

"Now she turns up. Where you been?" he said, by way of greeting.

"Out west, home. My father was sick." She wondered what had happened, but did not ask. She hadn't been there.

"He ok, now?"

"He died."

Jackie looked down slowly, looked at her sidelong, then full on. Quiet.

"Funny you running into me down here," he said. "I'm never around here anymore. Don't live in the project now. Moved uptown. You know, it's so quiet up there I can actually hear myself think." The surprise of this soothing discovery livened his eyes.

"Sometimes I just sit there, and listen to the quiet."

When Jane slips back into the present, the song on the radio is long over. There is a news report on the Aboriginal Justice Inquiry. A member of the Indigenous Women's Collective is saying the Inquiry hasn't been talking to the right people. The Inquiry hired a former Mountie to investigate the RCMP's work on a case in The Pas. A nineteen-year-old Cree woman named Helen Betty Osborne was forced into a car by four white teenage guys, sexually assaulted, stabbed with a screwdriver, kicked in the face and dragged into the bush outside the town.

To die there.

Jane pictures the bush country outside The Pas, a place she has been. Light November snow melting underneath the woman's slowly freezing skin, on the slowly freezing ground. Fifty-six stab wounds. With a screwdriver.

First, the reporter says, they took her to a cabin belonging to one of their families, but she screamed so loudly, fighting them off, that they drove on to somewhere more secluded.

Her mother said she could only recognize her daughter by her eyebrows. Said it in Cree.

White people in The Pas knew the names of those who did it within weeks of the killing of Helen Betty Osborne.

The former Mountie praised the investigation. It took the RCMP sixteen years to bring two of the four white men to trial. One was convicted. The woman on the radio offers a list of people the Inquiry should be speaking to. Listening to. Indigenous people. The Inquiry has only spoken to four. And twenty-nine whites.

Screamed so loud through fifteen years of silence.

They can't even find injustice, Jane thinks; how will they ever find justice?

Home sweet home.

Hate. Sophia used to talk about hate.

Hatred, she said. A Sophiaword.

"Hatred," Jane says aloud, and thinks about a glass of scotch, two ice cubes floating. About the soft skin of a faraway woman, the firm thighs of a once-upon-a-time man.

"Love," Jane says, as the radio announcer says something about a thunderstorm coming in from the west. She sees the stuffed pickerel above the mantelpiece, the Irish goblets below it. The empty overstuffed chair beside the cold fireplace. Inheritance. You come by it honestly.

Hate is the opposite of love.

Love is a mystery.

Jane stands and paces. A detective, seeking the ghosts that she suspects possess her. Paces. Counts.

One.

Hate. Plain as their hands raising screwdrivers, ramming fifty-six times through her terrorized skin.   two   three

four

It has always been here.   five   six   seven   eight

Plain as his foot, inside a warm boot, crashing down on her face.

Long long north November night.

nine

At least as long as we have.   ten

Plain as the silence that reigned in The Pas.

Sometime between November 13, 1971 and October 3, 1986, it became a crime, in The Pas, Canada, for a white man to murder a Cree woman.
eleven   twelve   thirteen   fourteen   fifteen   sixteen
Headline, front page, *Muddy Water Free Press,* three days earlier.
"CRUISING FOR NATIVE GIRLS CALLED COMMON IN THE 1970'S"
seventeen   eighteen   nineteen   twenty
As if someone didn't know. Everyday life in The Pas, in Muddy Water, in a thousand towns between Sudbury and Vancouver.   twenty-one   twenty-two   twenty-three   twenty-four   twenty-five
Lee Harvey Oswald.   twenty-six   Died in a prison cell, murder wrapped tight in a shroud of secrets.   twenty-seven   twenty-eight
Lee Scott Colgan. Traded immunity from prosecution for testifying about the long long north November night.   twenty-nine
"I learned to keep my mouth shut after the first time I was beaten." Lee Scott Colgan's ex-wife.   thirty
Evidence.   thirty-one   thirty-two
Testify, bear witness, attest to truth.
Without speaking.
thirty-three   thirty-four   thirty-five
" . . . why didn't they just drop her off at a coffee house, apologize and smooth things over? Even if Osborne had gone to police, would they have believed a drunken Indian girl, screaming hysterically in Cree?" a journalist wrote.
thirty-six   thirty-seven
Drunkenindian. Canadian English.
                                        thirty-eight   thirty-nine
Evidence.
A nation knows the answer to that question.
In your nervous system.
        forty
A good detective assesses the facts. Pieces them together. Jane paces back and forth. Cold stone hearth.
Canada, from ka-na-ta, Huron-Iroquois in origin, meaning "a spirit of community."
Nation-state founded in 1867 by an act of the British Parliament, a body of Anglophone white men.
Drunkenanglo, Sir John A.
Alcoholism is endemic in Euro-Canadian society. Anthropological study.
forty-one

Use the tools at hand. The evidence.   forty-two   forty-three
A jury of twelve—ten men, two women. All white.
forty-four   forty-five   forty-six   forty-seven
Founded on lava 2,000 million years old, hard-rock country where she
testified.   forty-eight   forty-nine
Jane stops, sucks a deep breath. The rhythm continues, her restless feet
on the worn, dusty carpet.
And justice delayed is justice denied.   fifty
Sophia knew that.   fifty-one   fifty-two   fifty-three
It's in the *Charter of Rights.*
          fifty-four   fifty-five
"Of course," Jane says to herself, "I would have believed her."
fifty-six.

Jane sits. It is quiet. So quiet. In the far distance an outboard motor starts
and Jane sees Phil, in a beat-up hat, sweatshirt and canvas pants, steering
an outboard at the back of a boat, a fishing rod leaning over the side.
Then she realizes it is a picture that used to stand on the bureau in her
parents' bedroom. It is hard now, so many years later, to imagine that
Phil and Sophia shared a bedroom. But there is a photo of a professional
man in his leisure clothes, fishing from a boat. There is the rough texture
of bedspread that belongs in a forest.
Evidence.
Opposites attract sometimes. It's chemical.
Sophia knew that.
Sometimes they repel.
Phil never quite realized.

When her job at the community centre in Toronto ended that long-ago
September, Jane gave Shulamit rent for October and November. She
kissed goodbye a nice Jewish man who had always seen that Jane
wouldn't stay with him and, without speaking, had let her know that he
didn't mind. Jane drove west, to see Phil. For a couple of months.

As the children play it, scissors cut paper.

Snip.

II

EVIDENCE

Love is a mystery I can't understand
But isn't it grand oh, isn't it grand

ANONYMOUS GRAFFITI,
women's toilet,
Albert's Hall, Toronto

Heat rising. Sweat and sunlight. Jane doesn't mind.

At the cabin, there isn't a telephone. Jane doesn't mind. The telephone has been ringing for years. The news has been good, bad, constant. Change has been constant. She is glad of the quiet, of nothing happening on the surface. She has a sense that the future is hidden in the past. Her past, and wants to find it.

Go quiet, still. Listen and cut. Rock to rock to rock to. Cut. Strong hands, big woman's hands, big as a man's, shove a saw forward and back. Into the wood. Inherit the earth.

Hand tight, grips, shoves a rough blade forward, rocks back. Shove forward rock back. Shove, rock. Rhythm. Fingers stiffen, bush bends bends bends sways cracks. Open. Light, air, motion. Continual repetitive relief. Rhythm opens the cloak. Breeze caresses, coaxes. Teases.

How long will she stay, cutting quietly? How long does it take to change history with garden clippers, a handsaw and earnest arms? Jane's gloved hand brushes away mosquitoes. Dank. Heat and muscle. She throws a bush onto the pile and thinks of a woman who might be waiting and a man who never would. Skins smooth. She wild, boundless, precarious, beckoning. He carved, careful, deft. Attracted and aloof. They are both far away, in the present. Shove forward, rock back. Jane is sweat and sunlight, muscle and bugs. Alone. She drops the saw, peels off her gloves and walks toward the lake, discarding clothing along the way. Heat rising. Mops her brow with a tattered kerchief, unzips her jeans and pulls them off hastily. Heat rising. He is wild, precarious. She is carved, aloof. Sunlight and sweat into water. Icy cool. They are far away. Jane doesn't mind. Heat rising. Icy cool.

Sophia knew a woman could weep for the suffering of others. Knew how to. She was born that way.

Phil knew a man had to push and shove to get a good seat. He learned it on the train to the beach in the summer, where he bought unused portions of day-return tickets from people going out and sold them to people who wanted to return. Phil knew that a day-return was cheaper than a regular one-way. Had to, to get a seat on the train to the beach.

Jane grew up believing that dignity was closely related to weeping and that every item from the grocery cart should be placed price side up on the counter, in order to read the price on the item and the amount the clerk punched in, simultaneously.

Phil was not a mangia cake.

Phil always did the "big" grocery shop. A morning spent touring bakeries, delicatessans, greengrocers; stepping off sullen prairie sidewalks into European oases. Sometimes Phil stopped for rounds at the hospital, and left Jane in a car thick with the richness of rye bread and challah; corned beef, pastrami, and salami from Oscar's; bratwurst and bochwurst from the German-Canadian meat market; parmesan, olives and coffee from the DeLuca Brothers; strawberries, cantaloupe and cherries from his sister-in-law's brother's wholesale.

Phil's medical practice spanned decades. In his company, Muddy Water was a cartography of bones and joints, of breaks and aches and stitches in passing strangers whom Phil greeted discreetly.

A smile of acknowledgement on the face of a woman walking past them. A nod, in return, from Phil. "Patient of mine, operated on her back five years ago," Phil's gruff voice in a stage whisper, his lips twisted exaggeratedly toward Jane's ear.

"Hi, Doc."

"Hello . . . Pin in his left elbow."

"Mornin', Doctor."

Nod. "Gout."

"Gout? Like Henry the Eighth gout?"

"Ssshhh . . . gout. Swelling of the joints. Says he doesn't drink but I can tell if he has with one look at his knees . . . Don't look back."

"He didn't see me."

Sophia did the everyday shopping. Milk butter juice toilet paper, things that ran out during the week. Things the kids ate, like pre-sweetened cereal, marshmallows, macaroni, canned soup, peanut butter and jam already swirled together in the jar. She shopped at the grocery store in the neighbourhood, buying the children things they'd seen on TV and requested.

"At least they'll eat it," she said. Sometimes they did. Sometimes they couldn't.

Sophia bought *The I Hate to Cook Book* from which she extracted expedi-
ent recipes. She made Chicken Marengo by mixing one can of cream of
mushroom soup and one can of tomato soup, pouring it over chicken
and baking.

Sophia thought of it as very North American. Convenient. One of her
small liberations.

Phil ate it if he didn't know what the ingredients were.

Phil's mother, Baba Edith, spoke Yiddish to her friends, English to Jane
and her brothers. When Jane visited, she listened to Baba Edith talking
on the telephone, the dense flow indecipherable, suddenly her own
name clear in the stream. Soon after that Baba would hang up. When
Jane went home, Baba Edith gave her special things to eat to take with
her. Jars of gefilte fish, cabbage rolls wrapped carefully in tinfoil, little
plastic containers of chopped liver. Jane watched quietly as Baba Edith
placed ingredients in her meat grinder and slowly wound the handle.
Pungent chopped white onions, a teaspoon of lemon juice, a pinch of
pepper. Chicken livers stuffed gently into the top, one at a time. Eased
out brown and soft.

Jane always thought of the packages Baba sent over as Phil's food.

Nobody else ate chopped liver.

On the flight over the Atlantic, Jane's younger brother Gene covered the
liver served at dinner with his napkin. "Liver! Plug your nose."

The family was going to Ireland for the Christmas holidays, to visit
Granny, aunts, uncles and cousins.

Sophia's family.

Jane was thirteen.

Sophia's parents, Granny and Grandfather, had separated in the late
1940s. Grandfather then took up with a woman Sophia referred to as
The Actress, giving the term a Victorian sense of scandal. Whether she
had ever acted or not was irrelevant to Sophia's family once Grandfather
had insinuated himself into her household. No one related to Grandfather knew, in fact, what the woman's profession had been, or even
whether she had had one. Granny and one of Sophia's sisters never
spoke of his existence, past or present. Sophia and Maeve, the other sister, plotted quietly to stay in touch, their attention focused on how to
maintain contact with their wayward father without disturbing those
who felt he should rightfully be banished from society.

One quiet Dublin evening Jane and Gene sat talking to Granny in the sitting room of Aunt Maeve's small house. In the hallway doors were opening and closing, but Granny's hearing was on the wane. Jane noticed Sophia and Maeve exchanging significant glances as they went in and out of the room. They were up to something, but Jane could not get Sophia's attention. When she finally succeeded, she was fixed with such a stay-put stare that she did, even when she heard them leave the house. Later, when Sophia said that Owen had met Grandfather, Jane knew exactly when. As she and Gene sat talking with Granny, Sophia and Maeve had slipped out with Owen to meet their father. Once and only once.

Much later, Jane discovered that some of her cousins didn't know Grandfather had ever existed. He had been expunged from family photo albums and stories; for them, he had simply never existed. As adults, it puzzled them that they had never wondered. "Grandfather" was not in their emotional vocabulary. They had never noticed it missing. A few years after Jane's family visited Dublin, a lawyer, whom The Actress had hired, phoned Uncle Charles. Charles was married to Aunt Maeve, the sister who did keep in touch. Grandfather, said the lawyer, was blind and broke. The Actress, a quiet grey-haired woman in her sixties, was ill in hospital and needed to sell her house. Grandfather wouldn't leave it. Uncle Charles and Aunt Maeve discovered a shrunken man alone in the dark in an empty house, thrashing about with a cane and cursing. Grandfather died shortly after. At the funeral, which they arranged, Maeve and Charles hid behind a post in case any of the disapproving family members were about.

Sophia said that whenever she went back to Ireland, for the first day she couldn't understand why she had ever left. By the third day she was dying to get out.

Baba Edith baked nothings. Barely sweet pastries so light that a bagful weighed nothing. Jane and her brothers devoured them. Sophia made Duncan Hines and Betty Crocker. Let the kids lick the bowl. "I don't bake," she said proudly. This saved her from of a lot of recipe conversations.

Sophia loved politics. Political talk made her cheeks flush, her eyes flash, her hands dance. She joined a socialist party in Ireland at the age of fifteen after announcing that she did not believe in Catholicism. It wasn't a renunciation; Sophia hadn't ever believed. In her first election campaign Sophia worked for Sean MacBride, staunchly Republican son of the staunchly Republican Maude Gonne, immortalized in poetry by Yeats

and in life by her years of struggle on behalf of Irish political prisoners. In the cabin in the Canadian woods, Sophia, with a glass of Scotch in her hand, read poetry and gazed into a fire in the old stone fireplace. *And I will arise and go now, and go to Innisfree*
She was watching the past in the present, watching the spirit dance in the fire.
Though spirit is a word Sophia didn't use.
After Phil died, Jane asked Sophia if she ever felt like she knew about things before they actually happened. Sophia looked surprised, caught out in some dangerous secret.
"I had an aunt when I was young, one of my father's sisters, who I was very close to. One afternoon I was at a movie and I felt this sudden chill, all over me. When I got home, I learned my aunt had died."
Jane was intrigued.
"Frightening," was all Sophia would say.

Phil wasn't in a wheelchair for years and years.
It was less than one.

Baba Edith's family came from Rumania, by way of Odessa. She told her children that one of her brothers had died of influenza while he was a student, studying to be a doctor. Actually, he had been killed by Cossacks, as a cousin later disclosed. Murdered in the street in an Easter pogrom. Jane's great uncle Yossl. Sharp winter-blue eyes, fine long-fingered hands for stitching. Edith's hands, Phil's hands, Jane's and Gene's hands, murdered in the street of a small town outside Bucharest. The waiting when he did not come home, waiting and praying, the family knowing, as the hours passed, knowing before they were told. The father putting on his coat as the first rumours of the pogrom wafted in. Pogrom, and where was Yossl?
Murder fixed the steel in those blue eyes of Edith's. Murder moved the family to Odessa, where steel became young Edith's will to have a positive view of life and a son who would become a doctor. After quiet years in Odessa, pogroms whirled again and the family left for England, planning to sail to Canada. Her father had chosen a much-heralded new ship, but young Edith pointed out to him that they couldn't sail on it, as it left on a Friday evening.
" 'It's *Shabot*,' I told him. 'We can't sail on *Shabot*.' You know what is *Shabot*? . . . So that's why we didn't get on the Titanic," Baba Edith told Jane. "Would have ended up in Davy Jones' locker."

Jane asked Phil what Davy Jones' locker was.

"The bottom of the ocean, sailors' graveyard. They made a musical about it."

Phil loved musicals. He had tapes of *South Pacific*, *My Fair Lady* and *The Music Man* that he played on his old reel-to-reel when the mood struck him. He sang along loudly.

Sophia preferred *West Side Story*. Her favourite number was the last song, in which Tony and Maria harmonize about a place, somewhere, where they can be together, voices soaring with hope as he dies.

A marriage punctuated by longing.

Sophia hated when Phil sang, particularly songs from his army days and "Hallelujah, I'm a bum."

"O-oh, I went to a house, and I knocked on the door," Phil began.

"Ugh," Sophia responded.

"And the la-dy said . . . "

"There was nothing funny about the Depression."

"How do you know? . . . Bum, bum, you've been here before . . . "

"There's nothing funny about poverty."

"I lived through the Depression, I worked at Silverman's Dairy for pennies an hour, got a raise when I showed Silverman how to skim the fat off cleaner, half a cent a day. And I considered myself lucky to have a job."

"You were lucky to have a job."

"*You* were a schoolgirl, at a convent school in Ireland. *I* grew up in the North End, a Jewish kid from the North End . . . Hal-le-lu-jah, I'm a bum, hal-le-lu-jah bum again, hal-le-lu-jah give us a hand to revive us a-gain."

Phil did not sing well, but he did it with gusto, which increased Sophia's exasperation. She glared down the dining room table at him, clearing the plates from an over-ample brunch of grapefruit, eggs, bacon, sausages and rye toast. As she disappeared into the kitchen, the children, Jane included, sang with Phil.

"Mad-a-moi-zells from Arm-a-teers, parlay-voo"

"Ugh," resounded in the kitchen.

"Mad-a-moi-zells from Arm-a-teers, parlay-voo"

"There was nothing funny about the Second World War," Sophia announced from the doorway to the kitchen.

"How do you know? . . . Mad-a-moi-zells from Arm-a-teers"

"Don't teach the children that. " Her eyes on a scalpel twirling in his hand as she retook her chair. The butter knife glistened in the late morning sun as it spun.

"Hasn't been ... " They sat end to end, stared face to face. " ... kissed ... " Three pairs of children's eyes fixed on the battle line drawn down the middle of the table. " ... in a thousand years ... "

"War isn't fun."

"Hinky-dinky parlay-voo."

"Why teach the children that war is fun?"

"What do you know about it? I landed at Normandy on D-day. *You* were a schoolgirl in a convent in Ireland."

"The Irish didn't fight in the Second World War."

"Really?" asked Gene, who had long lines of plastic soldiers strategically arrayed in his room.

"Still mad at the British," said Phil.

"I think I just might know more about my own country." Sophia grew indignant, one of her best roles. She turned to the children. "We did not wish to support the British Army in a war." Sophia, spokeswoman for the Republic. Maintaining a brave face despite members of the IRA who fostered dubious connections with the Nazis, those nationalists who still plotted by the Republican motto: "England's difficulty is Ireland's opportunity."

"Oh the sea oh the sea oh the glor-i-ous sea," Phil sang. Sophia picked up more dishes and hurried to privacy in the kitchen. "Long may it stay, between Eng-land and me."

With gusto.

It's a sure guarantee that some hour, we'll be free.

One day, when Jane was in her early teens, Phil and Sophia got into an argument over who had a smaller waist. Phil was bragging because when he was on a trip to Toronto, a friend of Owen's had lent Phil some jeans to go to a coffee house, and they fit. Owen's friend never admitted the jeans were too big for him, because Phil was so proud of fitting into them. It wasn't that Sophia was large; her stomach protruded because the muscles had split during her final pregnancy. She couldn't pull it in. She wore girdles until the seventies.

"Betchya my waist is smaller than yours," Phil said.

It wasn't.

Not long after that Phil claimed he could take a ring off anyone's finger, without cutting either the ring or the finger.

"My wedding ring won't come off," said Sophia, nonchalant. Sophia was good at nonchalant.

Slumped in a kitchen chair, Jane's attention was immediately piqued by Sophia's dissembling.

"Sure it will. "

"It won't." She pulled at it faintly.

"Let me have a look at it . . . Jane, get me some string."

Phil spoke as he did in the operating room, direct orders.

Jane found string in a drawer stuffed with superflua like broken candles, half-open boxes of dusty toothpicks, decks of cards a few short and envelopes scribbled with Phil's old shopping lists. Phil test-ran one end of the string under the ring on Sophia's finger.

"Ouch."

"I can get it off. Betchya five dollars I can get it off."

Jane tried to catch Sophia's eye but Sophia evaded her. Jane wanted to tell Phil the obvious, but it was, after all, obvious.

"You're on." Sophia had him where she thought she wanted him.

"And it won't even hurt."

"Better not." And off they went.

Jane heard yelps from upstairs over the strains of the CBC rebroadcast of the opera live from the Met in New York. *La Traviata*, Sophia's favourite. Then arguing. A pained Sophia asking him to stop, Phil ordering her bluntly to sit still.

"Don't move, goddammit—I'm almost finished."

"Oooowwwww! You're hurting me."

"Got it."

When they came down, Sophia's finger was red and swollen. The ring came off painfully, even with Phil's foolproof method. He had wound the thin string around her finger, beginning above her knuckle, then over the knuckle, and pushed it under the ring. He then unwound the string from below the ring, forcing the ring over her knuckle.

"You owe me five bucks," said Phil. "I won the bet."

Sophia got out her wallet, then held it behind her back.

"You said you wouldn't hurt me."

"I got the ring off."

"You hurt me."

"Jane," Phil's face reddened, he bellowed and commanded, "Jane's the witness. Who won the bet Jane?"

"Look at my hand." Sophia raised her empty and bruised finger.

"There's no ring on it." Jane, almost inaudible, apologized to Sophia's eyes.

Split decision.

"Marry for kindness, not for brains."

The wisdom of Sophia. Price paid.

In the humid after-rain Jane wanders to the rock where she first cut. Squats. And digs. Claws into the root. Fingers in soft brown dirt. Moist and loose. Pulling, slow, slowly, steady, steady, roots lift, run back along tendrils, pull free. Free. Dense sweet air so after-rain sugary. Moist. Thick with mosquitoes sodden leaves rolling moss. Soft solid and welcoming. If there is a home, it is this moment, inside the inside. Hands in earth, freeing it. Loving hands, rootless memoried hands, knowing hands, choosing hands. Where is that wild woman? Jane's fingers in soft brown dirt. Digging, slowly kneading roots free.

Home.

When Phil took Jane shopping, he added the grocery prices as the clerk punched them in, in case there was something wrong with the cash register. It pleased him to say the exact amount of the total before it appeared on the cash register, often startling cashiers. Phil tried to coax Jane into racing him to the correct total. "How much is it?" he'd say, or, "Sixty-one dollars and forty-five cents" and look at her expectantly.

Phil never could decide if Jane was too slow mentally to do it or simply refusing. She never said anything, just stood beside him and pretended to watch the prices come up.

So she never really knew, anyway.

Jane only ever added prices to be sure the money in her pocket was enough to cover the total.

She could do it very quickly when it was necessary.

Imprinted.

His pattern.

Phil liked to cook and bake. Baked Alaska, poppy-seed torte with lemon filling, couscous, lemon meringue pies, veal Marsala that he pounded earnestly with a wooden mallet, baklava, waffles with fresh-picked blueberries, Caesar salad, baked ham with pineapple.

"Your father's very interested in cooking," Sophia would say afterward, "but he's not very interested in cleaning up."

Doctors do not clean operating rooms.

One day Phil came home with a blender he'd just had repaired, intending to make gazpacho soup. On the wooden cutting board he set out tomatoes that had deepened from green to red, freshly-washed cucumber and green pepper with beads of water sliding down smooth skin. He peeled and sliced deftly, juices oozing into the wood on which he cut. He chopped herbs, releasing clean scents into the kitchen, squeezed lemon and lime, crushed garlic under the flat metal blade of a butcher knife. Then he methodically filled the glass pitcher, and fitted the pitcher onto the machine. Jane and Sophia sat in the dining room, reading aloud articles from the newspaper that were amusing or politically outrageous. Ignoring the aroma that drifted from the kitchen.

Phil pressed grind. Nothing happened.

"Goddammit! That son of a bitch doesn't know his ass from a hole in the ground. Trying to rip me off. Goddamn thing doesn't work. Doesn't do a goddamn thing. To hell with him." Phil threw on a jacket, "He'll make my goddamn soup." He thundered out the front door, in his hands the blender filled with carefully selected ingredients. "I won't be back without gazpacho soup." Car tires screeched as he drove off with his vegetables.

As Jane and Sophia silently watched him go, Jane decided Phil probably was crazy.

She was twenty.

Baba Edith met Zeda Max outside a theatre on Main Street in Muddy Water. Max, having roamed here and there, was working taking tickets at the moving picture show. Edith was walking by with her sister, as they did every week when they went to look at the fabrics and designs of the clothes in the stores. Edith was nurturing a dream of studying design in New York City. Steel resolve. Each week she looked at well-dressed mannequins, and at home she drew the design and elaborated on what she had seen. She cut paper, pinned and altered. Experimenting. Learning many ways to achieve the same effect.

Max said hello to the smartly dressed young woman with steel-blue determination in her eyes, bowed his head politely and saw Edith's sister place a hand firmly on Edith's arm.

"Don't speak to him. He's one of those *schlegger* Cammens."

They walked briskly on. Max watched their fine figures until they were out of view.

Edith was twenty.

A year later, Edith was working in the couturier women's clothing section of a major department store, handling the clothing she once admired on mannequins. During the day she adjusted skirts, jackets, coats and dresses to fit the figures of the wealthy ladies of Muddy Water, her mind persistently asking her to move a pocket, a tuck, or a dart, always wanting to perfect the design. When she purchased a length of fabric, Edith laid it on the wooden chest in the room she shared with her sisters, absorbed its details and read it with knowing hands before sleep. In the morning, she woke with a design in mind. High neck, back opening, long close-fitted sleeves, six covered buttons on each wrist.

By the time Edith married Max, she had become local buyer in the department. The manager wanted to promote her to U.S. buyer, which meant travelling to New York City. Dream city.

"Your Zeda felt I should be at home," Baba Edith told Jane, while a vision of New York City, 1918, with horse-drawn carriages through Central Park's early beauty, silks and satins, fine wools, weaves from all over the world, hung between them. "That was a good job for a Jewish girl, and I was the only one they wanted. But Zeda didn't want me to, so I said no."

Before the 1919 General Strike, Zeda Max was a member of the One Big Union.

Phil cooked Oysters Rockefeller. He sliced garlic cloves into a pan of melted butter and bread crumbs, added leafy deep-green spinach and sauteed lightly. Then he spooned it all carefully into open oyster shells, laid fresh oysters on top, squeezed lemon over them and slipped them under the broiler. It was the first time Jane ever liked spinach. She picked the oysters off the top and ate the rest. Eventually, Phil just bought shucked oysters each time, and reused the same shells, washing them in the dishwasher after use. The shells sat in the cupboard for months, sometimes years, between uses. Jane ate the spinach out of the frying pan, before it got anywhere near the shells.

Zeda Max had a stroke in the early fifties. Spent seven years as an invalid, in a wheelchair. While packing up Phil's house after he died, Jane found a letter tucked in a book about Israel that Phil had given to Baba Edith for her birthday one year. Jane saw her own handwriting in the book, " . . . and love from the kids," and had no memory of signing it. The letter was from the Muddy Water Electric Railway Company. After Max and Edith got married, Max drove a streetcar for them. It was about Max's pension benefits.

February 20, 1953

Dear Mr. Cammen:

We are writing to confirm the arrangements made concerning your retirement income. The amount will be $52.16 per month and will commence as of January 1. Since you chose a pension which, with the present Government Old Age Pension will give you a level income for the balance of your life, your company pension will be reduced to $12.16 per month as of April 1, 1964, when you will be seventy years of age. Should your death take place before that of Mrs. Cammen, then she will receive a pension of $19.75 per month from that date as long as she lives.

We hope you will remember with pleasure your many years with the company.

H. Macklin,
Retirement Committee

Zeda Max died in 1958. Baba Edith lived until 1975.

Jane imagined Baba Edith opening those cheques in her high-rise apartment across from the mall. Useless amounts mailed from the past, arriving monthly to the spotless one-bedroom with plastic covers on the floral couches, *TV Guide* and *Reader's Digest* in the magazine rack and mints in the candy dish. Baba Edith would stand on the balcony and watch Jane cross the broad treeless avenue and the expanse of the parking lot, to the supermarket in the mall. She would still be standing there, waving, as Jane made her way back, hoping her shopping was adequate. Fruit had to be squeezed and smelled, so that it would ripen on the day Baba wanted to use it. Except bananas, which had to be warm yellow, with no brown, and firm. The cash register tape, which Jane could not lose, had to match the prices on the food exactly. If anything wasn't just so, it was either back to the store for bananas without brown or fruit without bruises, or an extra trip for Baba Edith across the wide avenue, through the dangerous parking lot, to discuss the discrepancy in the bill with the manager.

"He's a nice man, the manager," Baba Edith would say.

Liberace, on the other hand, was "such a nice man." His hairdo the same as the ones Baba Edith and her friends got done at the mall. His fingernails, like his jokes, polished and shining. He was one of them. Accepted. And someone else as well. Those old closets.

In 1975, $19.75 bought one ten-ounce jar of instant coffee, one quart of milk, one loaf of bread, a pound of butter, a dozen eggs, two pounds of minced beef and the same of boneless, a couple of pounds of cooking onions, two seven-ounce tins of salmon, a pound and a half of liver, one six-ounce package of tea bags, two cans of cream-style corn, one head of cabbage, a dozen oranges and two pounds of bananas, leaving $1.97 for Baba Edith to purchase a five-pound box of detergent and a further $1.97 for an economy-size container of dishwashing liquid. All of which made it possible for Baba Edith to offer a friend a salmon sandwich with tea or coffee, or fry up a plate of corn fritters when Jane came for lunch, or make a little chopped liver for Jane to take home to Phil in a plastic container. Providing, of course, that her rent was already paid, that nothing was in need of repair, that she had a cupboard full of staples, that her apartment was furnished and fully equipped, that she didn't need to take a bus or a taxi to see a doctor or over to the synagogue on a Saturday morning, and that she didn't want to buy a newspaper, or post a letter, or even pick up a piece of fabric to exercise those agile aging hands and that furtive mind.

Zeda Max was one of twenty-five thousand workers in Muddy Water who went quietly home at eleven a.m. on May 15, 1919, according to the directions of the Trades and Labour Council. He and Baba Edith had been married one year, three months and thirteen days. Phil was five months old.

The days of One Big Union.

The days of the General Strike.

The Citizens' Committee of One Thousand, in quiet collaboration with the government, immediately organized against the strikers. Committee members lived in the neighbourhood where Jane later grew up, the neighbourhood where Phil and Sophia bought a house that had hosted Paul Robeson.

Jane imagined Paul Robeson stepping out of a grand old car, straightening slowly, to stand, tall and commanding, on their wide front steps. Paul Robeson surveying the green lawns and well-painted shutters owned by the people who wouldn't let him stay in their hotels. Houses owned by the sons of the Citizens' Committee of One Thousand, tended by women from the north-end neighbourhood where Phil had grown up, under the direction of the Committee members' daughters. Without doubt, Paul Robeson had seen it all before. Jane was still learning. She saw grandchildren of the Committee members in their private school uniforms each morning as she walked to public school.

Sophia believed in state education.

Until her children started to tell her what it was like.

She had never endured it.

When Jane was ten, Sophia was elected to the school board.

Later, someone spray-painted the name of Sophia's political party on the side of their house and nobody bothered to paint it over.

By then, Sophia had lost interest in appearances.

And all sorts of things were beyond Phil's control.

It was around the beginning of the neglect, but before it really set in.

The house was made of stucco and wood shingles.

And stone, limestone.

There was a fossilized fish on the front.

After Sophia left, it really set in.

The neglect.

At the cabin, caragana grew wild.

Word went out on Tuesday, the thirteenth of May, 1919. Strike vote passed: 8,667 for, 645 against. Walkout Thursday, eleven a.m.

Go home, stay home.

Eleven a.m.

All over Muddy Water, workers went home.

Telephone operators, hydro, water works, fire department, electricians, teamsters, followed by four thousand railway workers. Restaurants and movie theatres shut. Newspaper presses and streetcars stopped. By one o'clock the city was still.

Zeda Max went home and stayed there. There was excitement in the quiet, tension in the north end of the city. Five months earlier the sound of boots on ice had ripped open a frigid January night. Demobilized soldiers roamed the city from business to business, demanding that "aliens" be fired and returning soldiers hired in their place. The mayor and the police force followed behind, but chose not to intercede. The veterans rampaged through the north-end neighbourhood, smashing windows, kicking in doors, dragging Max's friends, Max's relatives from their homes, from their beds, from their dreams into the naked cold. They demanded to be shown naturalization papers, documentation of citizenship entitling the bearer to civil rights the ex-soldiers were violating. The "alien Huns" and the "filthy Bolshevists" had seen all this before.

And thought they had escaped.

Freedom from.

Danyluk, a neighbour of Max and Edith's, was pulled from his living room into the winter night. His glasses shattered on the crusty surface of snow as a boot forced his face down to kiss the Union Jack. For two days the riot went on, while the Muddy Water branch of the national manufacturers' association placed full-page advertisements in the *Muddy Water Free Press* pledging to "assist soldiers in their re-establishment to civil life." The association had hastily passed a resolution to replace "enemy aliens" with returned soldiers "wherever they are able and willing to do the work." And the provincial branch of The Returned Soldiers' Commission developed a survey, also advertised on a full page of the Muddy Water daily, asking employers, among other things, "Will you give preference to soldiers by discharging enemy aliens or other employees provided a soldier can fill the position?" No one formally defined "enemy alien" but any man who had an eastern European name and hadn't enlisted qualified.

Two days of riot, pogrom, invasion. An army in the streets.

The populace indoors, hiding inside. If they could.

Each day, Zeda Max was torn between risking the journey to work or losing the day's pay.

"Tomorrow, I will work," Max said.

"Tomorrow, I will boil the water as your mother did, and pour it from the roof on those Cossacks," Edith answered. But in the middle of the night, as they lay awake with Phil between them, they heard the silence. "Long live Rosa Luxemburg," Max said, for the soldiers' original intent had been to disrupt a Socialist Party memorial service for Rosa Luxemburg and Karl Liebknecht, two "Hun Bolshevists" who had just been assassinated in Germany. Rumours of the soldiers' approach had preceded them, and the meeting was quickly cancelled.

"And us, too," Edith said quietly. "God forbid we should die by Cossacks here." She got up to make Max's breakfast and lunch.

On the first day of the strike, a mass meeting of three organizations of soldiers gave complete support for the strikers. The three hundred members of the Strike Committee asked the police and phone operators to stay at work. By the second day of the strike the Citizens' Committee of One Thousand was formed and active.

Covert.

Supporters of the Citizens' Committee complained to city council. As one well-known Muddy Water suffragette wrote, "water pressure was reduced to thirty pounds, for that is enough to bring it to one-storey buildings and the *Western Labour News* stated that it is in one-storey buildings that the 'workers' live." Nellie McClung went on to say there "was something so despotic and arrogant about all this, that even indifferent citizens rallied to the call for help." The call from the Citizens' Committee. On the third day the Strike Committee met with the city council to discuss maintenance of essential services. Deliveries of milk, bread and ice resumed. Signs on the delivery trucks read "Permitted by the Authority of the Strike Committee," which proved to be too much for the Citizens' Committee of One Thousand. Their eyes read "Workers' Control, Soviet Government and Alien Enemies' Committee" on each passing truck. They pressured the mayor, who had agreed to the signs, and the city council, which then took a second vote on the issue, deciding to have the signs removed.

Still the strikers stayed home, venturing out only to meetings. Max began gardening. In the small backyard, he put a shovel into the black prairie soil, and weeded and turned, weeded and turned. That first year it was all vegetables, edibles. He built a chicken coop in the corner of the yard out of scrap wood, and traded three jars of Edith's dills for two chicks.

"There was more in those jars than two chicks," Edith told him.

"There's more chicks in these," Max answered, "and the dill and the cukes will be ready by August."

"God willing," said Edith, "and what until then?"

No one knew.

Sophia's ringless finger slowly healed. For a time, a ceasefire held between her and Phil. Until Sophia was ready. Then, the house in the south end, the house in the neighbourhood of the Citizens' Committee of One Thousand, the house that Phil bought with cash because he didn't believe in owing money, the house that Paul Robeson slept in, that the scared speed freak draft dodger from Kansas hid out in while his hair grew over his ears, the house where the wife of the prime minister with the bow ties grew up, the house where Phil let the lawn grow two feet high when Sophia took the children to the lake cabin for the summer, the house with the limestone base and squirrels running between the walls and a fossilized fish on the front, was put up for sale.

Sophia told Jane she was leaving September fifteenth. Said she was going to visit Ireland, and then England, and then she'd see. Going back.

Jane left for Toronto September first of that same year. She was just twenty-one.

A year and a half had passed since the argument they'd had. The argument that Jane couldn't remember.

A week after the strike began the federal ministers of labour and justice arrived in the town, escorted by members of the Citizens' Committee of One Thousand. Three days later the postal workers were told to return to work by ten a.m. the next day and sign an oath disavowing connections to the Trades and Labour Council, or be fired. The provincial and city governments gave the same ultimatum to their workers. On a dry summer evening, in the shade of oaks and elms in a downtown park, five thousand workers gathered. As evening cooled and moistened the air, the question that wasn't a question was decided. They would stay out. Max heard the news from Danyluk, as he traded two jars of *borscht* for a sack of seed potatoes.

"At least we can eat them," Edith said.

"A little sun and rain, and we can," Max agreed.

"God willing," said Edith, "we'll get *kreplach* and *kugel* for those two jars of *borscht*."

"It's a terrible scar, he's got, Danyluk."

"They left him two eyes, those Cossacks." Edith turned to go in, Phil cradled comfortably in her arms. "Now he's got two good jars of *borscht* to go with them."

When the old family house was sold, Phil moved to an apartment in another old house, just outside the Citizens' Committee's neighbourhood. An entire house meant too much work. He wanted something he could manage. After a few peaceful months Phil became embroiled in a dispute with the landlord about the laundry facilities, refused to pay his rent and was evicted.

The Citizens' Committee of One Thousand conducted its overt campaign against the strike through a daily bulletin called *The Muddy Water Citizen* and through advertisements in the newspapers that returned to publication after the ministers arrived. "The people must choose between the alien enemy and the flag," the advertisements read. "The alien enemy, who openly or secretly supported Germany and Austria during the war, who contributed money for bombs used in blowing up munitions plants on this continent, who danced for joy when the *Lusitania* was destroyed, who rejoiced over the long list of Canadian casualties. There is no room in Canada for the undesirable alien who insults our flag, intimidates our citizens and demands soviet government."

So said the Citizens' Committee.

No room for Baba Edith and Zeda Max.

No room for Paul Robeson.

No room for Helen Betty Osborne.

Two weeks into the strike, the federal *Immigration Act* was amended to permit the deportation without trial of non-British subjects charged with sedition. Days later, the *Immigration Act* was re-amended, to include those born in Britain in the earlier amendment. It had been discovered that the strike leaders were not "Huns" after all, but British immigrants. The second amendment passed the House of Commons and the Senate, and was signed into law by the Governor-General in less than an hour. The fastest passage of legislation in the nation's short history.

The Committee knew that hatred requires emphasizing difference.

English was the only acceptable language of patriots.

All other languages were different from English.

Suspect.

Your nervous system.

Upon receiving his eviction notice, Phil moved to a penthouse overlooking the Muddy River and the downtown where Owen worked. The moods and dances of the omniscient sky relieved the modern sterility of his apartment. Phil liked to watch the sky. He gazed out over the downtown and pictured Owen going about his day, imagining that he watched over the powerful as they exercised power. From his dining room table he could see the provincial legislature on the long lawns that stretched beyond the trees which hid the statue to the Métis martyr, Louis Riel. Hung by forefathers of the Citizens' Committee of One Thousand.

As the strike wore on, Max kept digging and planting. Sometimes in the late afternoon, as the heat thinned and mellowed, Edith would leave Phil sleeping in a basket in the shade as Max worked. If he woke and cried, their little world shook. Both would be at his side in seconds.

"Get a cool cloth, Edith, he's too hot."

"I'll get a warm one, not to disturb him so much."

In the heat of summer, the air conditioning collapsed in Phil's penthouse apartment looking out over the yellowed lawns of the legislature. Phil refused to pay his rent.

After two days of driving, north of Lake Huron, west by northwest along the north shore of Lake Superior, through pulp towns and mining towns, granite and fieldstone and pine, northwest again to where the shield opens out into prairie, past the sign marking the longitudinal centre of

Canada, Jane arrived in Muddy Water. The eviction notice had already been served.

Phil, Owen told her when she arrived at his house, was in the Hospital of the Holy Martyr.

Sophia hated martyrs.

"Martyrdom is like heaven," Sophia said, "it's a way of convincing people to accept what gets done to them on earth. Ugh."

Sophia hated Good Friday.

"On Good Friday," she said, "I would sit with my sisters in the dining room playing cards with my father, while my mother sat in the living room, in the dark, crying. At three o'clock, my father would lead us in to her and we'd each give my mother a kiss. Then we'd go back to playing cards in the dining room."

"Why three o'clock?" Jane asked.

"That's when Christ died in Ireland."

"What about Easter Sunday, what did you do for Easter?" meaning chocolate Easter eggs and fuzzy pastel chicks in baskets and wasn't Granny happy then?

"On Easter Sunday my sisters and I took egg cups, filled them with water and went upstairs. Our house looked out over the main road in the town. We poured the water on the hats of ladies going to church. Just a little bit, so they wouldn't be quite sure if it happened or not."

"What did Grandfather do?"

"Not very much."

"I mean for a living."

"He was an accountant."

"What was he like?"

"He was a chancer. He didn't do much, but he enjoyed himself. He went to jail after he was caught running guns for the IRA and I'm afraid, after that, he just didn't do much. He didn't seem able to care about anything, really ... " Sophia stared into the distance, into her father's face, into the blankness that had returned her mother's entreaties. "He was charming, though."

"What about Granny?"

"Your Granny taught school until she was seventy-five. She was dating someone else, first, you know, but then my father was just so charming, he charmed her away with him. The other man went on to a distinguished legal career, became a judge. Poor Granny."

As the caragana recedes, the landscape changes. Becomes older. Jane sees a tree that had been missing. That she had been missing. Exactly where it was. Slips into sounds, footsteps. Children running in the forest. Chasing. Hurrying past. Hiding. Branches, leaves rustling. Voices.

"Home free"

"Gene? Owen?" Jane walks to the tree. Wraps her arms around it and squeezes. Rough bark smooth wood. Stiff.

The first time Jane went to the intensive care unit in the Hospital of the Holy Martyr, her eyes kept straying to the screen where Phil's heart was blipping its rhythm. She was embarrassed. Because Phil seemed so well, talking and joking with her, while all around were people who were comatose. Because her eyes kept wandering from Phil's face. To the screen. Protection is the nurturing of strength, the cleansing of wounds that isolate and inhibit.

"They're springing me tomorrow," Phil whispered. "But I have to come back the day after for tests ... They ... they're thinking about surgery, a by-pass operation. If it's three or less than three valves, Strom can do it. If it's more, it'll have to be Lescaud, he's the best in the city."

Safety is not needing protection.

Smooth bark rough wood. Arms stiff. The children are quiet now. Jane releases. This, too, is home. This memory. How close it comes.

On June 9, 1919, the city council fired the police force for refusing to sign a contract that forbade them membership in any union. The Citizens' Committee of One Thousand began recruiting the "special police." Sons of the Committee from the Canoe Club, from the high school Jane attended fifty years later, backed up by sixty employees of the MacDougall Detective Agency, whose wages the Committee was later reimbursed, in full, by a grateful federal government.

Two thousand special police, "specials" as they were called, replaced 240 police.

On June 10, there was violence.

The first since the beginning of the strike.

"I put an offer in on a house," Phil told Jane from his hospital bed. "Go and look at it."

From outside the house appeared small and cosy, one and a half storeys of brick. As she walked in the door Jane knew why Phil wanted to buy it. Dark wood ran halfway up the dining room walls, oak cabinets had been built beneath leaded glass windows. A fireplace in the living room, a sun room on the front with French doors. She was walking back into the house in which she had been raised.

"I didn't think he'd be able to buy a house from a hospital bed," Owen shrugged apologetically, watching Jane pack a few weeks later.

"I'd rather live in a house than here," Jane answered, discarding ten dry and dusty oyster shells.

"He might want those." Owen reached into the garbage. Smiled sheepishly.

"I'm allergic to dust." Jane continued packing the box. She looked up. He was stacking the shells on the kitchen table. "Owen." She heard Sophia's tone-of-authority voice. "We'll be throwing those out." You're-just-like-your-father. Sophia's voice. They both heard it.

The first arrests came before dawn, on June 17, 1919. Six Anglophone, British-born leaders of the strike were accompanied from their homes in the fuschia pre-dawn light. Four eastern European men, active in the leadership of their new communities in Muddy Water, but not leaders of the strike, were also arrested. The strike leaders weren't alien enough. Emphasize difference.

All were charged with sedition and were to be held without bail, so that deportation hearings could proceed under the new *Immigration Act*.

The arrests broke the spirit of the strike. There would be no one big union for all workers. No collective bargaining across trades. No overt solidarity across the labouring class to parallel the covert upper-class solidarity cemented through clubs and societies and class-conscious marriages and the Muddy Water Board of Trade. In his garden Max dug deeper, digging beneath the anger that swept the neighbourhood, threatening to overtake his planting. Anger was dangerous. Danger was near.

"Danger is always near," said Edith firmly.

"There will be something, now there will be something."

"Always, there is something, Max."

The city government made a pledge to the citizens that the streetcars would roll. Max felt the whir of steel on steel in his bones. If he did not leave the garden now, the streetcar would roll without him. Roll on down Main Street. But no one, thought Max, is going to get on.

"An empty streetcar on Main Street," Max said, and bent to hoe.

A veterans' group announced there would be a silent parade in protest against the arrests, from the city hall to the suite in the palatial railway hotel where the federal ministers were staying. Saturday, June 21.

Shabot.

In the morning, Max left the garden. He was restless and went to synagogue. Edith stayed home with Phil, who she felt might be feverish from the heat. Temperatures had been in the nineties for days.

The streets were bathed in a hot bright quiet as Max walked. The congregation was small and agitated. Beneath the canting, under and over the prayers, Max heard steady whispers. "City hall, two-thirty ... Bob Russell, sure, Dick Johns ... stay the deportations ... the specials, the Cossacks, *nu*, all the same, we're still here."

When he left the synagogue, Max walked over to Main Street, crossed it, and walked south along his route, toward city hall. As he got closer he could see people gathering. Max kept close to the buildings, away from the street, clear of the over-excited and the anxious. Skirting the edge of the fever.

Steel on steel, a streetcar, rolling south behind him. Max's pace quickened, moving with the wheels behind him, wheels that the crowd ahead had not yet heard. As the streetcar lumbered by, Max's feet left the ground. The crowd surged into the street, chasing it.

"Scab!" "Scab!" A stick, flung at the passing streetcar, bounced wildly into the crowd.

Wedged between flesh and sound Max heard a second streetcar approach, struggled to get ground beneath his feet and force his way back onto the sidewalk.

Steel on steel. Tracks clogged with people. Max heard braking, through arms and heads saw the big car begin to sway and roll. See. Saw. People scrambled to shove and run. Steel scraping steel. A heaving ship in a landstorm. They couldn't topple it. Max eased his way back, pressing his full weight against bodies behind him. Wires fell from the cable, the crowd swarmed forward.

Glass cracked. Smashed. Clattered to the ground. Smoke.

Choking grey billows through shattered panes. Max backed away. City Hall loomed across the street. Another sound, from around the corner, from the south. Hoofbeats. From the avenue, around the corner, specials and Mounties, on horseback, charged into the crowd.

The crowd split. The street a parted Red Sea. Max on a wave that rolled to the sidewalk and broke. The Mounties hauled on the reins, reared the horses and turned. Back through a hail of rocks and stones. Max drove his elbows deep into bodies. Pushed and shoved for space in the crowd. Eyes on the road. Eyes always on the road. The Cossacks turned again, clubs drawn. Max felt his back up against a building, began easing his way along to the alley, forcing bodies forward when he could. The Mounties turned again.

"Scab!"

Max saw Danyluk heave a stone at a horse and rider. Saw a Cossack fall. Suddenly, something happening on the steps of city hall. The mayor, with a paper in hand.

"The riotact, the riotact, the riotact" skipped on passing tongues. The Cossacks turned again. Riding back. Eyes on the road. On their hands. Hands on, hands on, hands on. Guns. Max saw. Moving feet moving hands shoving pushing squirming. Back against the stone wall. Easing along the stone wall to the alleyway. Hands on the guns.

"Crackcrackcrackcrackcrack!"

Guns stop time.

An old man fell into nothing. The crowd dissolved into feet running for the alleyways.

Suddenly, Max thought of the garden.

"They're shooting!" "Scabs!" "Run fool, run!" "*Meshugina!*"

"Run Max, run," Edith's voice. Edith holding the baby, Edith opening the back door to find that Max was still not back in the garden. Run Max, run. And Max ran for the door that Edith held open, he ran for his potatoes, for three large jars of dills traded on a promise, for the *borscht* that he might never taste again, for the fine black earth soft and moist in his hands, for the child that sleeps while he hoes, for the woman who would calm these beasts with boiling water.

At the end of the alley, an Anglo special, club in hand, lifted it high and brought it down. A huge man took the blow, felt the wood smack his flesh with a dull thud. He fell, rose to his knees. "*Srăka!*" He swore in Ukrainian, covered his head with his hands and charged the special. As they collided, *schlegger* Max shoved a fist in the special's face and sprinted past them, running on to the bank of the Muddy River. He crept along the river bank, low through the tall grass, until its rustling drowned the sound of screaming. Walked cautiously up a back lane toward Main, dusting off his clothes. The street quiet. Dead quiet. Max smoothing his hair as he darted across Main Street, still patting it down as he opened the front door. Curtains drawn in the room where Edith cradled Phil.

"They killed a man," Max said into the shadows as his eyes adjusted. Edith didn't answer.

"It's over now." Max walked through the house to the backyard, gazed at the hoe he would draw through the earth another time. Bent, and ran a hand through cool black dirt.

"Give me the suit," he heard Edith say behind him. "Put on these. God forbid you should ruin your only suit." Max turned and saw Edith offering his gardening clothes, saw baby Phil asleep in the shaded basket.
"A man lives and dies for nothing, sometimes," he said slowly.
"And that," Edith answered firmly, "is a man who forgets he has children."

Thirty people were injured, eighty people arrested in the specials' dragnet on Bloody Saturday. A man died, maybe two. Maybe something else. Maybe the spirit of a movement was murdered, perhaps the innocence of a young city was trampled into dust on Main Street. The city divided into north and south. Versus. More arrests in the following days. Public protest forced the government to bring the strike leaders to trial, in spite of the provisions of the hastily amended *Immigration Act*. Four members of the Citizens' Committee of One Thousand acted as prosecution. Seven strike leaders received jail terms, three were acquitted. History has it that they escaped martyrdom by becoming electorally invincible politicians, founders of the forerunner of Sophia's political party.
History kept no record of the four eastern European community leaders arrested that same morning.
Disappeared.
The focus of difference had shifted.
There was the north end.
And there was the south end.
The Strike Committee agreed to end the strike in return for a government commission that would examine the conditions that led to the strike.
The workers lived in the north end.
The owners lived in the south end.
Five days later, according to the direction of the Strike Committee, Zeda Max climbed into a streetcar at eleven a.m. and felt again the whir of steel on steel. He eased the big machine along the rails, and drove for thirty-three years.

If you grew up in the north end, you could prove you had made it by moving to the south end.
Prove it to yourself.
That's class.

Four years passed after Sophia's departure, four years in Toronto, before Jane came driving back across the Canadian shield, on to the prairie, be-

I am nobody; I have nothing to do with explosions.
I have given my name and my day-clothes to the nurses
And my history to the anaesthetist and my body to the surgeons.

SYLVIA PLATH
Tulips

Love, hold dear, be unwilling to part with, be devoted or addicted to.
Something. Anything.
Life, pride, power, language, honour, yourself someone else a dog a cat a
budgie a rock a toad.
Caress or embrace with affection.
A teddy bear. A gun.
An activity. Strolling, dancing, singing, crying, fishing, drinking, swim-
ming, flying, whistling, dying.

Mystery, something hidden or secret, something beyond human knowledge or comprehension. A novel or film that proceeds from a death,
causing a story that already happened.

Lying in a hospital bed at Holy Martyr, balancing fate against will, Phil
decided to have surgery.
Tests showed that about thirty-eight percent of his heart was functioning.
All the rest was disease.
Sixty-two per cent.
Gambling on odds close to two-to-one against, Phil made his decision.
A relentless mind in a withering body.
How to save your own love, if you have to.

In tragedy, the protagonist faces a choice between parting with life hon-
our freedom community or love.
Always the wrong choice. Always a tragic mistake.
Based on a character flaw.
The flaw is essential, written into the character.
The choice is contrived.
By the state of relations.

As June ends the lakewater warms from frigid to cold. Jane swims after cutting. Her toes curl over the rotting wood at the end of the dock. Her legs bend and spring, she glides through air, with greatest of ease. Into water. Glides. Arm lifts, legs kick, roll, face to the sun, sky, air, warm and open, face warm, back cool, fingers stiff, throbbing. Voices somewhere. Mind. Memory. Swims, arms over, arms over, stroke, breath, stroke, breath, flip over and over and down. Bottomless depth, cool to cold. Where lurk monsters of childhood. Down here, prehistoric fish, dinosaur fish in a prehistoric lake. Old bones. Depth to surface. Choosing. Whether and how, diving and returning. Breaking the surface, air warm. Kiss the water, thank the air for blowing freely, the lake for not changing. Safe, familiar, past and present. Water is home. This water. This motion of arms rising and falling, this movement forward, floating, slipping, otter-like through water, dolphin-like. Slipping, flipping, floating home.

With an overnight frost, Muddy Water muted suddenly to yellow, gold and brown. The crisp preface to winter curled into her bones as Jane settled into the little house. Laid Phil's clothes carefully in drawers, hung his suits in the closet, arranged furniture from the big old house awkwardly in the small new one. The furniture was too big for the rooms, its grandeur useless and deceived. The bed that had been *theirs* smothered the room that would be Phil's. The carved chairs of the parents sat silent at each end of the oak dining room table.

Jane roamed the streets in Phil's little car, the city a backdrop, footage in a film she'd seen too many times to really watch again. Her bones knew all the coming scenes. She drove past the sleek modern synagogue nestled in the neighbourhood of the Citizens' Committee as the congregation gathered on Rosh Hashanah. Read books from his collection, from their collection on his shelves, ones she hadn't noticed before. Wondered when and whether to phone Sophia in the small house she shared with her new companion, looking out on the Atlantic. East toward Europe, where she and Bob had met.

Jane called.

"He's having surgery tomorrow."

"Why? Why would he?"

"How are things there?"

"Jane, why are you doing this? You don't owe him anything—get on with your life."

"Sophia, he's not my husband. I won't have another father. It's different."

Sophia sighed. "It's rainy, but warm. And the place is coming along well, really well. We've got all the rooms done, so now we're painting. And we had a lovely drive into Chester this morning, the reds and yellows are so beautiful. You really must come soon."

"Yes, I'd love to."

Jane's grandfather, Eugene, was a gambler, a card-player and a drinker. He kept fairly busy, for a man who didn't do anything. He had a mid-level civil service position, secured for him by a brother in the Cabinet. And there he stayed, in the little town, placing bets, cutting cards, taunting and teasing those with more demanding and less secure positions. Doling out his precious charm to quiet the squeaking wheels of life. Domestic strife. Grandfather liked to escort his three blond-haired daughters to social events and enjoyed making surprise visits when they summered at Castleconnel. Grandfather bought his daughters bicycles on a time-payment scheme, and neglected to pay. When the bailiff arrived he found that the bicycles were registered in the names of the children, who, as minors, couldn't be sued for non-payment. Sophia, the sister who later kept in touch, and the sister who did not, were able to enjoy their two-wheelers for the time it took the bailiff to revise the papers in Grandfather's name. And Grandfather's luck had time to raise a few pounds owing.

The man who shaved Phil made him laugh. Quietly, as his brown hands gently stripped hair from chest and legs, from anywhere on Phil's gaunt thinning body that the scalpel might have to enter. Jane waited, flipping through *Maclean's* weekly "Passages" column while the straight razor sliced away Phil's greying. Waited to see him again. She only knew much later that it was the last time she would see Phil, really alive. Fully himself.

After came the dreams and desperation, shadows dancing, the dead reviving, fantasies played in present past as the future walked away from one man's ending life.

Kindness, skilfully applied, can draw laughter out of fear.

On a Sunday night.

Monday. Slower than real time.

Heart surgery.

Hours of crossword puzzles in the hospital cafeteria, Owen pacing floors halls stairs long corridors of inside outside as six hours became seven became eight nine ten eleven and finally twelve.

"Never really know what you're dealing with 'til you open 'em up." Phil, a surgeon's surgeon.

Jane solving and solving.

Words diagnostic.

At the end of the day, Phil, in post-operative intensive care.

Comatose.

The air crisp and cool. The room humming with the energy of complex machinery. Phil sprouting tubes. In the corner a group of Hutterites, praying around a bed. A man in it.

Tuesday. Sporadic. In and out of time.

Surgery on his left thigh.

Vein collapsed from the pump that beat for his heart on Monday.

To save his leg. Circulation.

Held Phil's cold hand.

His eyes opened. Saw Jane.

Squeezed his hand gently.

"Hi."

Clear plastic tube feeding oxygen in. Depressing his tongue. He squeezed back faintly.

Wednesday. Continuous present. Linear.

Phil woke. Slept. Woke. Slept.

Jane sat in the little room where family was allowed. Watched a Hutterite woman knit. Thought of taking up knitting. Waiting, for the phone to ring her, for another walk into the cool, to watch and squeeze.

Wednesday morning she saw his toes. Dark and blue.

Wednesday afternoon, toes blueblack.

Years later, outside the Royal Ontario Museum, an Iranian woman collecting money for surviving victims of Shiite fundamentalism showed Jane pictures of feet in a photograph album. Charred toes burned with electric prods. Jane donated quickly, wanting her to close the book. Phil's toes reflected in the glass door as she hurried into the museum.

The phone rang for the members of Dr. Cammen's family.

A doctor, tall, youngish, stood in the hallway as Jane walked toward the intensive care unit. Male. Pale.

"Mrs. Cammen?"

"Jane—daughter."

"Could I reach Mrs. Cammen?"

Jane held his eyes with hers. "No." Wished she was taller. "You can speak to me."

"Gangrene." She knew the word before he said it. Janedaughter of the surgeon's surgeon knew the story before he said the word. Cowboy story. Script written into her bones.

Only one man for the job.

One doctor Phil would permit to amputate his leg.

And only because he couldn't do it himself.

In intensive care, the Hutterite family was gathered again around the bed at the far end, in the cool air they wept and prayed while an elder read from the Bible. Jane watched Phil sleeping, looked at his toes, moved her gaze along the dying leg. And left.

Left the hospital, drove through the scene in which sun glints on the river framed by the bridge that crosses from the French community to the English, through the scene where the last dying leaves blow calmly, any day slowly ending.

To Owen's.

In a strict patriarchy, power passes from the eldest son to the eldest son. The power to make decisions. Final authority.

In a changing society, those losing power cling to its oldest forms.

"They have to amputate," she told Owen. Crying, he poured brandy for them both. Jane sipped and watched the scene where his son cries, pulls himself together and takes action.

"We'll have to phone Friesen." Watched him dial and speak, nodding appropriately, standing off to the side, out of the focus.

Jane drove Owen to the hospital.

Stood beside him as he spoke to the doctors, reciting the lines about how Phil would agree if Dr. Friesen said it was necessary. She knew the previous scenes which established Dr. Friesen as the only possibility, because he worked hard and well, because several months each year he treated people with leprosy in a faraway place that was as warm and wet as Muddy Water was cold and dry, because Phil knew his young faithful hands, because Phil had trained them. They were the closest hands to his own. She knew, too, the painful scene where Phil had abandoned his desire to accompany Dr. Friesen to the land where he amputated leprous limbs, having come to the realization that he, himself, was too ill to be useful.

Jane watched on as Owen spoke quietly to Phil, knew the look on Phil's face that was blocked by Owen's body. Knew the words that Owen said from behind his strained demeanour.

Watched Owen hand Phil the toy that they used to communicate in the crisp air, a plastic sheet on a child's clipboard, that they could use and re-use. A fake pen.

Knew that Phil scribbled badly, "Call Frank Friesen."

Watched Owen's mouth form the words, "I did."

Knew that what Phil wrote next, what Owen showed to her and then to the doctor wanting consent, was a scrawl that said, "If Friesen says it has to go, it has to go."

A broken heart.

Knew that even if she had done exactly what Owen had done, it would not have been the same.

Eldest son of the eldest son in the autumn of a patriarch. Rational learning. Roles born into. And she, the connection to the ground. Roots, emotion, feeling.

In a strict patriarchy, men and women are opposites. Strength is a characteristic assigned to men. Weakness is a characteristic assigned to women.

Weakness is vulnerability.

Strength is invulnerability.

In a strict patriarchy, men maintain power through not exhibiting weakness. Women maintain vulnerability through possessing and acknowledging emotion.

In a strict patriarchy, some opposites attract.

Others remain in opposition.

Cowboy stories. In the bones.

In a changing society, those losing power cling to its harshest forms. Those who move beyond those forms live with a strength drawn from abandoning the logic of opposites.

Thursday. Yom Kippur. A man out of time.

Frank Friesen said it had to go.

It went.

Down to the river where they throw the money in, emptying their pockets of the sins.

Down to the Muddy River where life begins again.

And death goes on.

Roll on muddy river, roll away.

Roll away sins and roll away money, while old man river wastes away.

He don't say nothin'.

He just keeps rollin'.

Away.

While Jane was in Muddy Water, Shulamit went to visit her grandmother in France. Her other one, who wouldn't join her grandfather in

Golder's Green before the German army arrived. Leaving Germany was enough. Over the phone Shulamit told Jane that her grandmother stood on the balcony of her apartment in the small town in the south of France, screaming in French at Shulamit, as Shulamit walked back to the market with unacceptable vegetables.

Jane laughed.

A few weeks after the phone call, a postcard arrived in Muddy Water from Shulamit, in France. It was a painting by an artist named Ben. The painting was plain black with white lettering reminiscent of Miro's script. The writing said "mourir c'est facile." On the back Shulamit had written:

> J.C.:
> Couldn't resist sending you this card.
> It's unbelievably pretty here, palm trees
> and what-not. <u>All</u> my relatives talk
> <u>all the time</u> of THE GRANDMOTHER and live
> in her shadow. I'm counting down the days
> 'til I go back to Paris.
>
> xox Shula

Phil fished, weekends with the boys. Friday evenings they drove east into Ontario, to Ellen and Jack's. Phil met Jack when Jack was injured at work on the great Canadian railway. Phil helped Jack with a compensation claim and Jack traded the rail gang for guiding sportsmen through the rich lakes of the Rainy River system. The Wabigoon River. Until mercury poisoning was recognized. Jack told stories spoofing rich Americans, Yankees. Like the one about the hunter who shot a moose, showed it off all over town, and arrived at the border to go back home, with his moose tied to the hood of his car.

"What the hell do you think you're doing?" said the customs officer.

"Taking this Canadian moose I shot home."

"I see," said the customs officer. "That one a doe or a bull?"

"Don't know—it's a moose," said the Yank.

"Hope they got their share of milk before you shot it, fella."

"Had to give all the money he paid me to the farmer," said Jack, laughing.

Sophia and Jane stayed in the city when Phil, Owen and Gene went fishing. Relaxing in the calm that was the house without Phil's temper. Emotional violence, Sophia called it.

Manipulation.

Castigation.

Suffocation.

Every trick in the book of control through tantrum.

"The hellitis   to hellwithyou   to hellwiththosebastards and that sonofabitch   don't give agoodgoddamnwhattheythink   don't give a goodgoddamnwhatyouthink   who asked you to think   don't think just do   you'reanass   you'reanasshole   she'sanasshole   he's anassholethatdoesn'tknowhisassfromaholeintheground   thatprickI wouldn'twalkacrossthestreettopissonhim   shitshitshitandmoreshit jesush.christyou'restupid   goddammitthatsonofabitch   you sonofa bitchshoveitupyourassso I told him toshoveituphisass   told her to shoveitupherass   told them all to fuckoff take one step closer and I'll shove this up your ass, Jane."

Brandishing a barbecue fork.

Sophia did not believe in physical punishment. Did not believe in spanking children. The children were not spanked. Not hit slapped punched molested strapped. Ever.

Sophia believed in non-violence. In the Reverend Dr. King, Mahatma Gandhi, the Quakers. Civil disobedience. Spent each Mother's Day at the Muddy Water memorial to the Great War in a candlelight vigil. Believed in peace, freedom, sleeping in late, kindness, poetry, escape, existentialism, laughter, dignity, loose dresses, democratic socialism, Nice'n'Easy number 106 until it turned her hair purple, opera, feminism and a drink before dinner.

Lady Bountiful, satirized on the editorial page of the *Muddy Water Free Press* for lobbying to increase welfare payments. For increasing payments to a man who lived in a wood shack without electricity, to a mother of four who wanted her children to have boots for school. Travelling the province to hear the appeals of those denied sustenance in the country with the fifth-highest per capita income in the world. Gavel in hand, appointment secured by the election of her political party.

In Pukatawagen, Picwitonei, Swan River, Churchill, Thompson and Dauphin, in Minnedosa, East Braintree, Cranberry Portage, Cormorant, Binscarth and Russell. In town halls and restaurants, Legion halls and commandeered taverns, Sophia listened and saw.

A parade of the dispossessed.

Poverty.

Lived in wealth.

Cradled the gavel, empowered and constricted by law, looked for cracks in the gold dome of power.

The golden boys.

Pushed on the cracks.

Abandoned the logic.

Abandoned girdles and Phil, Thursdays at the hairdresser, the neighbourhood of the Citizens' Committee of One Thousand, a wardrobe of knits,
satin and furs, the cool cedar closet with a rack filled with hats, three
grown children, the battlefield dining table she bought cheap at an auction, the Waterford crystal she brought when she came. The twenty-six
years when she honed her vocation.

When her party lost power Sophia saw the axe looming, denounced the
firings, and left before hers.

On a plane, with one suitcase.

Owen sent her half the proceeds from the sale of the house.

"Men," Sophia quoted, "get more conservative with age. Women get
more radical."

Magic is the art of influencing events by compelling the spirit.

Jane never saw Phil raise a hand at anyone, until he was dying.

Phil of the hair-trigger temper, shrill explosions, the outbursts of terror
that became Nazi armies in her childhood dreams.

Terror begins at home.

Until he was dying.

Max went to the *schvitz* every Sunday. He took Phil when Phil was a
child. In the *schvitz*, the neighbourhood steam bath, Max cleansed himself in good Yiddish gossip and oil-sweetened steam from boughs that
slapped his skin. Seeping through to the bones. Each Sunday he went to
visit his sister Miriam on the way home, to talk over tea, with an eye on
her chill-hearted husband and his mind on the state of Miriam's
thoughts. Miriam was what clinicians later labelled manic-depressive.
She spent thirty years in an institute for the mentally ill. Some said they
wanted to send her home at one time, but Miriam refused. Didn't want
to freeze in the chill love of her husband. Stayed to her death.

One Sunday they walked along Aikins toward Aunt Miriam's, Max held
Phil's hand in his own, and wondered if the ground was soft enough to
warrant turning his garden. Six-year-old Phil saw a teenager shove a
bearded old zeda to the ground. A light sweat rose on the hand that Phil
held, but Max kept walking. Said nothing. Pace constant. Walking by.
Max flung a punch. Flattened the young attacker. Kept walking. Pace
constant. Holding Phil's tender hand.

Granny saw the first Thompson gun that the IRA smuggled into Dublin. The provisional army. It was under the bed in the house on Leeson Street, where Granny and her sister debated republicanism and nationalism with young men they might marry. The previous day some Catholics had been surprised outside a factory as their shift ended and hurled into the Liffey. Jobs filled by the Prods. The next day, that gun waited at the gate.

Sprayed retribution for a hundred years.

In love and hate.

Once his amputation was done, Phil never walked again.

Except in dreams, Jane's dreams.

Standing with a peg-leg on his stump, balanced on the metal railing of a staircase in a walk-up apartment building. Phil jumped. Jumped again. Pounding floor to floor. Pounding and clanging, peg-leg on railings. Down down down down. Driving his pain into each watching child. With each leap Jane thought he would die, hoped he would die, ached as he landed full force a floor down.

Relentless.

When Jane was recovering herself, after he died, Phil walked through her nights along a beach, through pale fading light. Silent, his long body naked and blanched, along the sand through day in night, day in night, water lapping soundless on the shore. Empty sky, empty water, deserted beach.

Wake don't wake wake don't wake. Walk until walk until walk until walk.

Walk through a year, until dissipation.

After cutting caragana, Jane sometimes walks the small beach at the end of the road. Pale sun drifting. Quartz pebbles sparkling. Draws her hand to pocket. Water high, rough wood adrift, remnants of docks and boathouses float idle. Ice heaved and buckled, thrashed the shoreline one stunning day in May.

The little beach is ringed by buoys that mark a line boats do not cross. Line of safety. A sign, "Water at the buoys is forty feet deep." Lake crater. One hundred and fifty million years since a meteorite careened into solid lava. Rock on rock in a spinning world of water and stone. Creation. Space time contiguous. The meteorite thirty-five metres across. Perfect sphere vaporized on impact. Vaporized. Dust. Nothing but this hole reshaped by 150 million years. Glaciers grinding smooth lava rock, discarding sand clay gravel. Quartz to glitter in evening sun. Water to run a hand through.

Jane could call Phil's voice tomorrow, if she wanted.

Or Sophia's.

But not both at once.

Hands that rest in water. Cool, light water. Floating. Reach for sand. Dig. Pile. Fling. Sand over trees dock across the water flying. Hands that cannot touch their flesh.

Or hold their hands.

Or bathe Phil's bedsores.

Or brush Sophia's soft thin hair.

Her hands feel the loss. Jane's hands that cut, dig, saw, stiffen. Ache. Reach for quartz in sand, memorize trees, re-learn the patterns of moss on rock.

Soft deep tender rough, calloused, callousing. Gloves thinning. Hands that can. Cut and love. Hands that long, unsure of the depth of distress. Hands that cannot rest on the small of either back, and stroke it gently, until tension dissipates.

That cannot brew espresso coffee so delicious that Phil makes her a gift of his espresso maker.

Or bring Sophia fresh orange roses to a small flat off Portobello Road.

They can cut caragana. Pull, saw, bend and break. Listen to rocks and memorize the breeze. Jane can walk on lava, 2,000 million years cold, bend to pick quartz pebbles and arrange them in her room. She can watch the fire dance with a glass of scotch in her hand, add prices faster than a cash register, and smell a fruit to know which day it will be ripe. She can listen for voices night and day.

But she cannot stop the longing of her hands.

And so she cuts. And walks.

And mines for quartz inside her memory.

Memory, *memor*, mindful.

Remember, *rememorari*, call to mind.

Call and listen. Mindful is memory. Loons that mate for life, lapping water, croaking frog beneath the window. Rocks that will not quiet will not move. Balance neglect and caring, call the past within the present, cut back the shroud and study on the shield. Listen. Voices on the wind. Whispers, shouts. Lightning and thunder. Rain. Jane is up and running, leaving the lonely beach behind, running up the old cut-through path between cabins and water's edge, beneath pines, over roots, past the old pump and up to the road, down the hill, around the corner sharp to the right and there is the cabin, tucked further down, sagging and aged. Sprints up behind the woodshed, picks up shears and saw, stuffs gloves in her pockets. Laughing, runs for the cabin. Sheet lightning flashes. Illuminates pines, cabin and lake. Beauty sudden and sharp. Split-second relief. Hyper-real, more alive than life. This is mine, Jane thinks, because I have seen it. Screen door slams behind her, Jane peels damp clothes, huddles in soft towels. Lights flicker and dim. Out. Shaft slaps burning light sky. Out. Darkness rolling in on thunderheads. It's just a storm, Sophia is saying. Dry off, kids, get the kerosene lamps. Jane does. Lights two. So bright. And the smell historic. Thunder rolls, rains rattle on the roof. Kerosene burns. Jane lays a fire and lights it, too. Wraps a blanket around the towels and feels her own skin against them. Her own skin. The woman, she was there, had been, when Jane called. Her words strong and tender over the miles. Present. But was she waiting? Still?

Patronage once meant the same as protection. Under the care of a patron, *pater*, father.
"Come and visit," Sophia had said from a villa high above the Mediterranean.
"I'd love to, Sophia, but I'm a student, I don't have the money," Jane answered in Toronto.
"Just ask your father. He's got lots."
"No."
In a strict patriarchy, possession rests with the father. The first son, the progenitor, inherits the father's right to possess. Everything is done for the good of the family. Which the father owns, and defines.
In a strict patriarchy.
Those losing power shield themselves in the armour that once offered protection.
After the amputation, Phil came off the respirator and began to breathe on his own. He scowled when Jane entered the crisp oxygenated atmosphere.
Yanked out the tubes that punctured his body.
Intensive care madness.
The intensive care staff tied his hands to the bedrails and postponed the skin graft to cover the stump on his amputated leg.

Sophia came to Muddy Water, with her Bob.
Stayed with her friend Georgia and skulked around town. Her first visit since physically leaving Phil four years earlier.

Muddy Water, Phil's town. Where he grew up. Where his family lived, his friends, where his children were attending at his bedside. Her children.

Where Sophia had always lived with him.

Sophia decided to get her fur coats out of storage and give them away.

Phoned the furrier, who asked for proof that she owned them. She had stored them there from thaw to frost for twenty-odd years.

These last years she hadn't been paying the storage costs. Phil had.

The coat off your back.

Sophia phoned Owen.

Owen phoned the furrier.

Sophia got the coats, and the picture.

Nightmares realized.

"Someone phoned." It was Sophia. Frightened.

"What do you mean, someone phoned? " Jane knotted the belt on her dressing gown in the corridor of Phil's little house.

"Someone phoned and asked for Mrs. Cammen. No one knows I'm here. Georgia asked who was calling and they hung up. I think it was your father."

"Maybe it was the fur storage."

"I think it was your father."

"Sophia, he's not capable of calling."

"How do you know?"

"So-phia, he's in intensive care."

"So? Are you there?"

"His hands are tied to the bed." Knots tight at both ends.

"You're not there."

"Sophia."

"He'll never leave me alone. Never." The woman he had tried to strangle.

"Soph, please, Phil is not capable of making a phone call." A chill on the line at the mention of his name. *You are the enemy.*

"Georgia has to go to work, and Bob's gone downtown."

"Gene and I will come over." Gene had come to Muddy Water from Toronto as Phil's complications set in.

Jane told Gene about the call.

"I'll get dressed," he said quietly.

Sophia's eyes wide and furtive when they arrived at Georgia's.

"I'll stay here with you," Gene assured her.

Jane went on to the hospital, wondering if Phil really had phoned.

To remember you have to forget. Then call memory to mind. Call it from forgetting.

Without forgetting, the past is a continuous present.

Phil was moved to the step-down unit. Post-surgical, less intensive intensive care, for recovering patients.

He refused to eat.

A doctor cut a hole through to his stomach and put in a tube.

Liquid food poured in on a regular schedule.

Feeding time.

Phil pulled out the tube.

The staff tied his hands to the bedrails.

The hands that wanted to die.

"Jane, quick—go over to the counter, pay the bill and take me home."

"It's not a hotel, Phil."

"Pay the bill and get me out of here."

"You don't owe them any money. All this is free."

"I'm so thirsty and hot. Go outside, round the corner and get me a nice cold beer."

"Phil, you can't have beer, you have to eat."

"I'm so thirsty, Jane, I'm so-o-o thirsty. Just one cold beer."

"Phil, you haven't eaten anything. I can't give you a beer. I'll put some ice in a cloth and you can suck on it."

"I'm tied to the bed."

"I'll hold the cloth."

"Untie my hands."

Owen walked in.

"Owen," said Phil, "you gotta help me. I'm not rational."

Inside a strict patriarchy, very late in the autumn.

Georgia had a party for Sophia and Bob.

While Sophia went to six plays a week in London, ate taramosalata on Crete, met Bob, moved to Orkney and ran a creche for preschoolers while Bob taught, her political party had regrouped and returned to power.

With women in the Cabinet.

Sophia's old friends.

Georgia's party was a strange assortment of people who only knew each other through Sophia. People who hadn't seen each other for a long time. People who'd been through falling-outs in Sophia's absence, so long ago that they weren't avoiding each other anymore.

Jane knew all of their names, some of their faces, a few of their children.

Sophia worried about who would come. Who would shun her. Who would do both. She was grateful for each person who walked through the door.

"You know what Marion said?"

Jane knew, she had heard her say it. Marion was the minister of education.

"She said, she had the glory, but I broke the ground. That she wouldn't be there if I hadn't run first." Tears in Sophia's eyes that she turned away to wipe.

"Sophia, I knew that."

"But she said it, don't you see, she said it. I broke the ground. She didn't have to."

Jane's hand on the warm small of Sophia's back.

Sophia and Bob left Muddy Water.

Testify. Bear witness to.

Remember. Bear in mind.

Weekends are noisier. Jane hears the summer fun of children and teenagers, hears the "cottage life," once so familiar, as a backdrop. She tunes it out, it is the soundtrack to a story that is happening somewhere else, somewhere long ago, when people lived in families, did things in groups. Jane's past. She doesn't notice when a car engine comes close, expecting to hear it continue on by. Looks up only when car doors close heavily and a young voice asks, "You sure she's here, Dad?"

Jane glances up from cutting, sees Owen and his son, Jeremy, walking toward her. It startles her. Not to see someone walking down the path to the cabin. Company was always expected. That someone would come walking down the path to the cabin was always part of Sophia's lakeside tradition. What startles Jane is the realization that she is no longer alone. It is awkward to have people here in her landscape. Even familiar ones. Especially, perhaps, familiar ones.

"Hi."

"Hi." Owen smiles. Both look relaxed, both look younger than Jane feels. Suddenly Owen seems tense. Jane follows his gaze to the cabin as Jeremy runs down the slope toward the water.

"You've cut quite a lot," Owen nods toward the growing pile. "It looks really good."

"Yeah," says Jane, "it feels better." She rubs a gloved hand across her sweaty forehead. Sees Owen bend and pick up the saw. Stops as he bends a long caragana bush and begins to cut.

She taught him, too, Jane thinks. Taught all of us.

Push pull push pull. Jane watches Owen's hand move the saw. Quickly, hastily, urgently. Jane tenses. Too quick, those movements. He'll cut himself. Something will break. Push pull push pull crack. Stem snaps. Flies toward the pile.

Jane watches the man bend and begin again. Bend. Push pull push pull push pull snap. Bend. Watches, lifts the clippers. Her gloved hands on the wood. Snip snip cut. Thin, reedy stems. Incessant, insistent. Low low low to the ground.

Watches the man bend and saw. Pull. Push. The man, brother, Owen.

"Like a beer?" she says finally, dropping the small branches she has just cut onto the pile.

"Sure. Thanks. I'll just be a minute."

The cabin is dark after the brightness outdoors. Cool. Jane opens two beer bottles, drinks full from one and sits. Owen is standing at the screen door.

"I'll just check on Jeremy," he says, standing there.

"He's probably at the water. Here—have a beer." She holds it out to him.

"We're just staying with some friends over at Granite Lake," he says. Still standing outside the screen.

Jane watches him. Realizes he isn't coming in. Stands with a beer in each hand.

"You don't come down here anymore, do you?"

"Not for years."

"Want me to bring you this?" She shows him the beer.

"If you would."

She walks over to the door. He opens it and takes the beer from her hand.

"What is it?" she asks him.

"Voices."

Jane laughs quietly. "Come in."

"No. I hear voices in there." His shoulders begin to hunch. He seems to be disappearing into himself. Jane can see the Owen Cammen that mourns.

"Sorry. That's why you don't come here, huh?"

His shoulders hunch further, Owen closes his eyes. Nods.

"Come on," Jane pushes the door open. "Let's find Jeremy."

"He's, uh, he's probably at the water."

"Yeah."

They walk around the side of the cabin and down toward the water, carrying beer, pointing at trees and bushes. A maple sprouting where Jane has cleared, buttercups where wild grass is coming in. Jeremy is sitting on a rock with his feet in the water.

"It's cold here—way colder than that other lake," he says as they reach him.

"Well, it's a very deep lake," Jane tells him.

"The lake was created by a meteorite, Jeremy," Owen adds, "ages ago."

"A meteorite?"

"Yep."

"From outer space?"

"Yep." Owen smiles. Good things come back, too, Jane thinks, enjoying Jeremy's fascination.

"Gee," Jeremy kicks at the water, splashing idly, "all the interesting things have happened already."

Jane and Owen laugh.

"Want to go for a swim?" Jane asks. "Did you bring your suits?"

"Actually, we came to invite you over to Granite. We're barbecuing and I think some people will be water-skiing. I'll bring you back later if you want."

People, barbecues, water-skiing, Jane thinks. Holiday stuff.

"Come on," Owen urges, "a little company won't kill you."

"Yeah, come on," says Jeremy, "we'll have fun."

Fun. "Ok," Jane answers, "as long as you promise fun. I'll bring my car and follow you."

As they drive away, one car behind the other, Jane has a sensation of a long cord stretching out behind her, connecting her to the cabin and the bush surrounding it. Unfurling gently. Light as air, solid as a rock. Flowing like a river in spring.

Jane's earliest memories of Baba Edith were of a stout woman, with combs in long brownblack hair. She can picture Baba Edith with rounded breasts and full hips, standing at the mirror brushing out her long dark hair, parting it cleanly in two without checking a mirror, winding each half carefully up to the roots, then sliding a comb in each side. In the house. The house with the giant white peonies. Before the apartment.

Before Zeda Max died.

She has no earliest memories of Zeda Max, no memory of the man who loved to garden, who didn't stop until he had to. Until he couldn't anymore, because of the stroke.

Couldn't stop.

Father to son, father to son.

After the Depression, after Phil got his scholarship to university and then medical school, when a worker wasn't just dust on the rails, Max began growing flowers. He still grew cukes and dill for Edith's pickles, and sweet peas and beans that he coaxed up the fence. But he walked out the back door and picked up the hoe because of his flowers. For bulging white peonies, for blueviolet irises in June, for tiger lilies blooming orange and black, for six-foot-high sunflowers towering above him.

The household in which Jane grew up had no religion. It had moral philosophy. Noblesse oblige and the self-made man. Open discourse among all ages, talk of self-determination, anti-imperialism, Canadian nationalism, Quebec nationalism, compensation, unionization, government health insurance, social insurance, stories of J. S. Woodsworth's refusal to make Canada's entry into World War II a unanimous vote in the House of Commons, proposals for nationalization, government auto insurance, family law reform.

With contradictions.

J. S. Woodsworth abstained, Phil enlisted. Because of what Hitler was doing to Jews.

"If I thought you kids needed religion," Sophia said, "I'd send you to the Unitarian Church."

Packing toys in the basement to be flown to needy children in the north. "Needy" was one of Sophia's words. Materially needy, she meant. Boycotting South African products, grapes, lettuce, Chilean products after the CIA murder of Allende, Spanish goods until the demise of Franco. Saran Wrap because it was made by Dow and Dow made napalm. Kraft mayonnaise, Jane never knew why.

Sophia had never believed in Catholicism. She despised it instinctively.

Phil didn't break kosher until he was twenty-three.

The family celebrated Hanukkah and Christmas, Passover and Easter. At home, family ritual. A Christmas tree, no angels, a menorah lit without prayers, Easter a hunt for hidden chocolate eggs. Only Passover had any meaning beyond the material. It had story.

One evening Baba Edith was visiting, just before Christmas, when Jane was quite young. A Christmas tree stood decorated in the living room, tinsel and angel hair that made Jane's arms itch for hours afterward. Coloured lights on the tree. But never on the house. Jane was in the kitchen humming *Away In A Manger,* which she had learnt at school, wondering how cattle lowed.

"Jane," said Sophia, in an urgent whisper. "Don't sing Christmas carols while Baba's here. It's insulting."

"But doesn't she know?"

"That's not the point—you have to respect her feelings."

"Oh . . . Da-da-da-daah-dee-dee."

"Don't even hum it." It was hard to stop. Possessed by the demon spirit of Christmas, Jane avoided Baba Edith until the little tune stopped humming itself through her voice.

"Aren't you Jewish?" asked the orthodox cousins who'd just moved from Regina, seeing the thin pine gaudy and glowing. They were arriving to celebrate Phil's birthday, December 27.

No one answered.

Sophia railed against the constraints of Catholicism, against the Pope's edict on the pill, the lack of divorce and birth control in Ireland, the role of women in Catholicism and Judaism, against religion as a form of social oppression.

Phil bought ham to bake for Easter, bacon for weekend brunches and lavish presents at Christmas, and memorized his role in a nephew's bar mitzvah syllable by syllable, his Hebrew forgotten.

One Saturday morning a graduate student came to interview the children for her thesis on cross-religious marriages. Jane and Gene sat with the student in the dining room. "Where did Moses find the tablets?" the student asked.

What tablets, Jane wondered.

"Mount Sinai," said Gene.

"What's the Holy Trinity?"

"A church downtown," said Jane, who had seen it while shopping.

"The Father, the Son, the Holy Ghost," Gene answered. "It's a Christian concept."

"What about Mary, isn't she in there? . . . Mother Mary comes with me, gets us into heaven, little bee, little bee," Jane hummed.

"That's *Let It Be,*" said Gene.

"I know, I changed it. Too sappy. Anyway, what about Mother Mary, the cattle lowing, she isn't even in the manger in the song. And Baby Jesus never even cried."

"So?"

"So, she must have been right there or he would have. She's always in the store window displays."

"Nativity scenes," said the student. "Who crucified Jesus?"

"Ponch-us Pilot," said Jane. She'd seen *Jesus Christ Superstar* and formed her own conclusions.

"No," Gene countered, "he washed his hands. The crowd that gathered to condemn him was Jews, but the Romans were in control of the state."

"And Judah spilled the beans," Jane interrupted, "but he had to, or no resurrection, right? So he did everybody a favour."

"Ju*das*." Gene tried to ignore her. "I'd say the Romans, really, the government of the Roman empire."

"The Vatican's in Rome," Jane countered.

"That wasn't 'til later." Gene munched on a sausage.

"Oh, yeah, *Ben Hur*—the Christians and the lions." She'd seen it in Dublin with her cousins. "Ben Hur's mother gave Christ water because he was nice to her even though she had leprosy. I think she saw him rise up."

"No one saw him rise up."

"They did in the movie. 'So it is written, so it shall be done.'"

"That's *The Ten Commandments*," Gene corrected. "You're in the wrong testament and the wrong movie."

"What?"

"*The Ten Commandments* is from the Old Testament. The New Testament is the story of Jesus Christ. It's supposed to be written by his followers, who were the first Christians, really."

"Oh, yeah ... like *Jesus Christ Superstar*—When I'm old I'll wri-ite the Bible, so you'll all think about me when I'm gone," Jane paraphrased the song.

"The Jews believe the story of the Old Testament," Gene explained, eyeing his last sausage, "but they don't accept that Christ is the Messiah. They're still waiting." The student wrote copiously.

Jane pictured Baba Edith waiting on her balcony, peering across the shopping mall parking lot. "I think Ben Hur becomes Christian near the end of the movie. Sappy. And Moses should never've gone to the desert. If he hadn't been anti-Semitic, he wouldn't have been so shocked to be Jewish. He wouldn't have felt he had to go slave in the mud, he could've just hushed it up until he was Pharaoh and then freed the Jews. That way Nefertiti wouldn't have had to marry Yul Brynner, who she hated. Very inconsiderate."

"That's not quite how it goes in the Bible. And anyway we wouldn't have Passover," said Gene.

"Well, you got something there. How come you know all this Bible stuff anyway?"

"I've been reading it." The student scribbled hastily as he talked.

"Like a book?" Jane was astonished.

"Yeah, like a book. Read with eyes, words in the mind, remember reading Jane?"

"Ha ha. But it's wrong, Gene—why read it?"

"It's one of the founding books of western culture."

"Well, I looked at it once. Didn't get too far. I don't see how people make so much of it. I mean, the whole story of Cain and Abel is just a line. And Cain slew Abel. So? It doesn't say what anybody looked like, or what they felt like. It's just the lord this and thou that and smote this and plague that."

"Which one did you try?"

"Which one what?"

"Which version of the Bible?"

"King James, I think."

"Try the Old Testament. It reads better."

"I think I'll pass."

"This is all very interesting," the student cut in. "Just a couple more questions, if you don't mind."

"Sure," Gene laid into the last sausage.

Jane shrugged, still thinking about how Gene could stand to read the Bible.

"Do you keep kosher?"

Jane laughed. Gene looked closely at the sausage on his fork. Looked at the student, but she was still waiting.

"No," he said.

"Do your hands sweat at night?"

Silence.

"I don't know," said Gene flatly, "I'm sleeping."

"Buckets," Jane added merrily. "The sheet's soaked every night."

After the student had left, Jane asked Gene, "Did you ever try that thing about god shaking the curtains?"

"Wouldn't work anyway."

"Why not?"

"Well, if god's omnipotent, why would he bother shaking your curtain?"

Jane never tried, just in case.

Eventually, they took the tube out of Phil's stomach. The hole needed to heal. He was moved to a private room.

"What's that, Phil?" Jane asked, walking in.

"A bocxs of chocolates." His speech had begun to slur.

"Who brought them?"

"You know, what's-her-name. That I didn't take to the dance. You know, my mother and her sister didn't talk for a year after that. It wasn't really me. Mother told her no without asking me. I wouldn't have minded. Promise me you won't do that."

"Do what?"

"Fight with your brothers."

"Phil."

"I just want you all to get along."

"What if they fight with me?"

"I just want all my children to get along." He began to cry.

Autumn tightened around her.

"We get along, Phil."

"Gimme a chocolate."

Jane opened the box.

"Phil—they're half-gone."

"What's-her-name ate a lot before she left."

"Right."

"Gimme a chocolate."

"Did you eat anything else today?"

"The food here is shit. Gimme a chocolate. They're my chocolates—no one gave them to you. You're just trying to control me 'cause I'm sick. A poor sick old man."

Jane walked to the window and stood, watching the rain fall.

"Uuuhh!" Phil lurched forward and began to vomit. Thin brown liquid. Jane bolted. Caught him. Held him leaning forward, so he wouldn't choke. When he seemed to have stopped, she let go and ran to the nurses' station.

As they rushed back into the room he was gagging. Uniformed white surrounded the bed, asked her to leave. Jane was still standing outside the room when Owen walked up.

"Where's Phil?"

She explained and slumped into a chair, closing her eyes, trying to find calm.

"They're doing a tracheotomy," Owen's voice said above her. She opened her eyes to blame in his.

"I held him forward so nothing would stick in his throat," she explained.

"Well, that's exactly what happened." He snapped out the words.

I just want
you all
to get along.
Later that day Jane saw Phil back at square one. Intensive care unit.
Arms by his sides, impossibly still. A small hole in his throat, with a tube
coming out. Completely so totally motionless.
Still lifedeath.
I just want
Her knees buckled
all of you
going down she grabbed her shins, held onto a crouch
to get
breathed as deep as she could
along.
Falsified air.
In the small waiting room, a social worker came looking for Jane.
"Are you the girl that had trouble in there?"
"Pardon?"
"You know, seeing someone very ill can be very difficult for some
people."
Jane smiled. Strange apparition, some people.
"I just got a little dizzy."
"Have you been into intensive care before? It can be hard the first time."
Peering into Jane's face. Placed a hand on Jane's knee.
Go away. Jane closed her eyes, raised a hand to her brow.
"Yes, I have. I have been in there before." I've been in here, I've been
down the hall, I've been to the intensive care two floors up, I've whiled
away hours in the cafeteria, I've held the cloth with the ice cubes, I've
mopped his brow, I've arranged his house, I've driven day and night to
get here and been dragged directly to this hospital upon arrival by Owen,
because someone had to take over worrying, had to be responsible for
caring, someone had to slip into the space Sophia escaped. Everything
required it. Family. Hospital. Social workers. The whole damn system.
Everyone.
Jane opened her eyes and the woman was gone.

In a strict patriarchy, men maintain power by insisting that women show
caring, give comfort, soothe wounds, assuage anger, and then devaluing
emotion as weakness.
In a changing society, those drawing strength from new patterns feel the

reimposition of the strictest forms as an alienation from themselves.
Slow spiritual death.
In a causal philosophy, the agent must be identified.
A box of chocolates.
In a philosophy of emotions, expectations must be assigned to the person
that generated them.
Phil wanted to know his family would be alright.
Owen wanted to know his father would be alright.
Made Jane their agent.
A box of expectations.
Slice your way out.

Jane phoned Shulamit.
"He's back in intensive care."
"What happened?"
"He ate some chocolates and threw up. Something caught in his throat.
They had to do a tracheotomy."
Shulamit waited.
"I let him go. I was holding him, then I thought—what am I doing? This
is a hospital, it's full of people who know what to do."
"So?"
"I guess I should have held him longer."
"Why?"
"So he wouldn't have choked."
"How do you know he wouldn't have choked?"
Jane was silent. "I don't."
"That better?"
"Yep. So how's Toronto?"
"The same. Colder. Crawling with droolers."
"Droolers?"
"Like what you just did. Dripping all over. Droolers. I went to an open-
ing."
"Yeah?"
"Boxes. A whole room full of little boxes."
"What do you mean, boxes?"
"I mean boxes boxes. Small wood boxes, maybe eight inches across,
painted inside, made into rooms—living rooms, dining rooms, bed-
rooms."
"Good?"
"Drool. Decoration. All they're doing at the art college these days. I mean

how interesting is a living room?"

"Well, if you think about it, it could be interesting."

"Drool."

"As in a dying room."

"You're drooling again. Why only one room, then, if it's for all of living? That's trite."

"How about a drool room?"

"You got it. With poodles that group used to make."

"The poodle-heads? I always thought they looked like those old statues of Beethoven and Bach."

"Don't give me Germans. They look like poodles."

"We used to have a poodle. But you couldn't usually tell that it was. One time Sophia took it to get trimmed and they shaved it so clean it was embarrassed. It hid under the couch for days."

"You talk to Sophia?"

"She was here."

"Really?"

"Completely paranoid."

"She doesn't like me."

"It's not you. It's your intensity. You remind her of Phil. You remind me of Phil."

"Get lost."

"Well, energy-wise, anyway. Sophia spent twenty years longing for calm."

"I'll be calm when I die."

"I'd take it a bit sooner," said Jane.

"Drool."

"And I'd fill it with ruckus."

"That's better," said Shulamit. "Interesting ruckus."

"Poodles."

"Cats."

"I'm allergic."

"No boxes, no drool."

"Got it. And thanks."

"Drooler."

They hung up.

Air sweet. Light burning redorange black treeline. Dark and calm. Safe. Water to the edge of the earth. Still. Soundless. Feet slap quiet along linoleum, screen door snaps gently on old hinges. A large body shifts on steps facing the lake. Settles. Watches. Light drifting through the trees, framing emotion.

Jane wakes from a dream of city life. Commotion. A work dream. Everyone wants something. Jane arranging and arranging. Organizing. By nature Jane is an organizer. From time to time she is also one by profession. Prone to being called in to some small but vital social agency on the verge of collapse. Able, sometimes, to find the strands of new beginnings. Social, far from the life she is leading here. Half-awake, she sits up. Hears someone move on the front steps. Phil? Watching the sun rise? Bare feet slap quiet, screen door snaps gentle.

"Jane. Sorry I woke you. Isn't it beautiful?"

"God. I thought you were Phil."

"Spending too much time by yourself."

"How'd you get here, Gene? Bus?"

"Yeah, bus from Toronto. Walked in from the highway. You've done a lot of work out back."

"Yeah, here, too. That's why you can see the rocks there, and grass up there."

They walk down to the water, survey the dock.

"We should rip it up," says Gene, "it's dangerous."

"Yeah," says Jane, non-committal. Although she knows it is dangerous, she is not ready to part with it, yet. "What about the crib?"

"We can't move it."

"Not all of it."

"Yeah, I guess we can move some of it. Some of it's rotted anyway. See, over there, where it's more sheltered. If we rebuild there, the ice won't hit as hard when it thaws."

"Mmm-hmm. Come on, let's get some breakfast."

"Actually, I could use some sleep. That's a long ride."

"How long you here for?"

"Just four days. Have to be back at work by Monday."

"Ugh."

"It's the best I could do. It's nice just to be here."

"Yeah. It is nice. I'm glad you came. Wanna cut caragana?"

Gene laughs. "I was kind of planning on a vacation. Yeah, sure. It's really overrun everything. Cabin could use a little work, too."

"Yeah, but it's one or the other. And I'd rather cut the damn caragana. The way it is now, you can barely see anything."

" 'Cept trees."

"Even those."

"Come on, let's eat."

"Maybe I have been here too long by myself." Jane is quiet as they walk back up to the cabin. Something is happening. I can feel it, she thinks. Screen door slams gently on old hinges. Big feet slap quiet on linoleum. The inner room is cool and dark. Gene slumps into an arm chair. Jane goes into the kitchen and fills Sophia's old percolator with lakewater from the tap. Pours coffee grinds in the top, plugs it in. Switches on the radio and sits down in the armchair beside Gene. Both chairs facing the cold stone of the fireplace.

"It's a great fireplace, eh?" Gene stretches his arms out above his head. Closes his eyes.

Jane nods, relaxed. Closes her eyes, senses the life beside her. Relaxes more. Someone is here. The coffee is brewing. The radio is predicting clear skies and a high of 33 degrees. Centigrade. Must be 90 or so. Nice heat. CBC cuts from the weather to Joni Mitchell, raised on robbery on the Saskatchewan flats. Jane remembers listening to old Joni Mitchell with Marie. That wild woman. "Marie," she says quietly.

"Marie," Gene mumbles sleepily, "isn't she the woman you brought to my party?"

"Yeah."

"She's nice. You seeing her?"

"Uh. Maybe."

"You sure you haven't been out here too long? Coffee smells good."

"Well, maybe. But I just, I just don't want to leave yet."

"Not much point in getting crazy, Jane. It's not all it's cracked up to be."

"No—it's just the opposite. It just takes a while—that's all."

"Ok, I'll butt out. Anyway, she is nice. I ran into her on the café strip on Bloor last week or the week before. She said something about moving to the coast, I think."

"Yeah, she's thinking about it. Isn't everybody, these days?"

"Yeah. The boom is driving all the best people out of Toronto. Can't afford it anymore. Soon there will only be real estate agents, people who work in restaurants to wait on them, and tellers in banks to count their money."

"I don't know—it can't last forever. People will run out of credit and the bottom will fall out. It'll quiet down soon. Want some coffee?"

"Sure. I'll get it. You want?"

"Yeah. I'm glad you're here."

"Yeah," says Gene. "It's so great here."

Feet slap quiet on linoleum as Gene walks through the kitchen. Jane leans back. Rests. Loneliness is a tiring companion. Breathes deep. Air sweet, still cool. Water to the edge of the earth. Still. Soundless. A cool night heating into a hot day. Silent heat creeping, burning water to air. Water cool, ready. Homebound with Gene.

Granny lost more than one teaching position. She was punctual and orderly, well-informed, competent. And solidly behind the Provos. The provisional army. The IRA. The army of liberation, freedom fighters throwing off the yoke of colonialism.
But Granny was still teaching in the 1960s.
Teaching Irish history as she knew it, had known it. Lived it. Her husband in jail for a year. The year Maeve was born, her years of moving surreptitiously around the country, with husband and newborn, for he was known and marked, an easy target for the British Army and its spies. Riding the train up to the north, the baby swathed in her arms, past the farms where Irish lived on Irish land as tenants of the British, the lord's land on which Irish tenants could not set foot without removing their shoes. When the rail lines were cut, after the Treaty split the country into civil war, she and the infant Maeve huddled soundlessly upstairs in the house on the border, when soldiers came knocking. Where her mother in-law, related to soldiers on both sides, kept two separate sets of family photographs. Changed them hurriedly as soldiers approached, blithely dropping names they would recognize as she offered the sherry, surviving by understanding how those men thought. The matriarch.
The history that Granny had taught.
That earned her dismissals. A graceful, straight-backed woman who believed in God, woollen underwear and the Provos.
Until her dying day.

Phil's affairs were frozen in place.
"Couldn't you use the power of attorney?" Jane asked Owen. The power of attorney that Phil had suggested they get before his surgery.
"Well, there's a little problem there."
"Don't tell me. I can guess."
"I thought I'd get it if we needed it."
"Remember the girl scouts."
"I didn't want to rush into anything."
There are those who believe that preparations for the worst possibilities will ward off trouble, and those who believe such readiness will simply bring it on. Owen had Sophia's superstitious streak, and sided with the

latter group.

"Well, now there's a mortgage to be paid."

Driving the lawyer to the hospital, Jane tried to prepare him for Phil's state of mind. His altered consciousness.

"If he doesn't know what he's signing, I can't do it," the man said.

Box shrinking like Phil.

Owen met them at the hospital.

Phil signed the power of attorney, made out to Owen, as Phil had requested long before. They had been doing business together for years. Stocks and investments. Tax shelters with acronyms only accountants can pronounce.

Jane drove the lawyer back to his office.

Jane took in the mail. Opened the bills. Deposited Phil's disability pension cheques in the bank. Shopped for groceries, cleaned the house, made out the cheques to cover the bills.

Owen signed them.

A structure under stress relies on entrenched patterns.

The phone rang in the small house.

"How's Phil?" asked Owen.

"Ok, I guess, the hospital didn't call."

"You didn't go there today?"

"No."

"What the hell do you do all day?"

"That's my business. I don't visit Phil on your behalf. Go yourself."

"My time is more valuable than yours."

"To you. Fuck off."

Hung up.

Counted the minutes while he talked to his wife.

The phone rang.

"Sorry. It's just I'm working so hard."

"He asks for you all the time."

"I'll try and make it tomorrow."

She knew he just couldn't stand it. It was impossible for Owen to acknowledge that Phil was dying. To slow down and spend time with him. So much was supposed to happen before Phil died. A good marriage, a marriage of respect, a solid place in the world, a beautiful home. Grandchildren. Phil was to share that. Become an old man. Owen was hurrying, pushing time as hard as he could to get it all done, to provide Phil with the circumstances of an old age, in lieu of the reality. To save Phil's life, Owen had to move faster than time, because if you can move faster than time, time is essentially stopped. Relativity.

Phil was moved to a medical ward.

Needles all day.

Refusing to eat.

But not everything.

Sometimes Phil's sister-in-law Ruth brought him little plastic containers of chopped liver. Baba Edith's recipe. He'd eat that.

Then nothing.

Phil's fondness for food originated in Rumania, a place he'd never been. In a small town, not far from Bucharest, where Baba Edith and her sister, blue-eyed and blond-haired, went to a convent school and sang carols each Christmas in the choir. When pogroms spilled blood in the streets they left for Odessa, where Edith's sister trained to be a wigmaker. That's why she was hired at the department store even though everybody knew they didn't hire Jews. Baba Edith began work in Muddy Water in a sweatshop, then sewed piecework in a small factory that made collars. Edith's sixteen-year-old hands deft and accurate. Fast. She became the pacemaker for the factory, setting the standard by which all the workers were paid. When the factory went under, the owner went to friends in the haute couture department and spoke on Edith's behalf. Edith learned English in haute couture, promoted to local buyer, choosing fabrics for the wives of the Citizens' Committee. Hemming their dresses.

Stitching invisible.

Jewishness too.

The Muddy Water Electric Railway Company reportedly had the same policy when they hired Zeda Max.

But he had no beard, no accent and experience. They couldn't tell by his name, it sounded almost British.

Before he drove a streetcar in Muddy Water, Max drove a streetcar in Minneapolis.

Max had first left Muddy Water to see if the deed to the land his father had in Saskatchewan had lapsed. On arriving in Canada, Max's family had settled in Lipton, a fledgling Jewish farming community in 1905. After a year they gave up and moved to Muddy Water, where Max did eight grades of school in four years, and learned to speak English fluently. The land, Max discovered, had been sold for taxes. Max's father was born on a farm in the western Ukraine, which he lost when the Czar made it illegal for Jews to own land. He moved to the Pale, where all Jews had to live. Max was born in the inn his father and mother kept, where they sold liquor to Poles and Ukrainians and gave free rooms to Jewish pedlars, who walked from *shtetl* to *shtetl* to sell a ribbon, a few buttons, or a spool of thread from their packs. Max's father was an agent for an absentee Polish landlord who lived in Moscow. Each year Reb Haskell Cammen got a special pass, allowing him to travel beyond the Pale to Moscow and pay in the rents. Reb Haskell, six feet tall, bearded, kept a well-worn board with fresh nails behind the bar.

For subduing unruly customers.

A Cammen *schlegger* like his son Max.

The inn had one window. On the second floor, above the door. When the Cossacks attacked, his wife Reva poured boiling water and sent them running.

In the new country, they could own land.

But Reb Haskell had lost interest in farming.

After discovering that the land was a lost cause, Max went on to Alberta. He was in Edmonton when the Great War started and tried to enlist. He was refused. After a time, he took the train back to Muddy Water, where he was hired as the ticket-taker at the theatre and saw Edith walk by, refusing to say hello to him. He also saw the spark in her eye, and the way her sister warned her off.

Max got himself introduced to Edith and asked her out.

Once a month they dated, for a year.

Then the government brought in conscription.

That's when Max went to Minneapolis.

If the army didn't want him when he was ready in Edmonton, he didn't want them now.

He wanted Edith. So he left for Minneapolis, where he learned to drive a streetcar.

Eventually, Max came back to marry her.

A month later she was pregnant with Phil.

Max got a job with the Muddy Water Electric Railway Company that didn't hire Jews, because he knew how to drive a streetcar.

And how to be invisible.

On the medical ward, after the tracheotomy, Phil shared a room. When Jane walked in he was eating and his roommate was sleeping.

"What's for dinner?" She asked. Phil was eating something a violent shade of green.

"Lime Bavarian Cream."

"Good?"

"Yes, get me another one." Jane hesitated. "Go on, just go down the hall to the nurses' station and see if you can get me another one."

A yellow-uniformed nurse walked in.

"Did you take your pills yet, Dr. Cammen?"

"I'll take them if you get me another one of these." He nodded at the empty container in his hand.

"You have to take the pills first."

Phil put the pills in his mouth.

The nurse left the room. Phil spit the pills back into his hand.

"Phil!" Jane was disgusted.

"Wait and see if she brings it."

When the nurse came back with the Lime Bavarian Cream in hand, Phil stuffed the pills back in his mouth.

As he ate the second dish, Jane sat down and read him articles from the newspaper. Paused, looked up and saw he was sleeping, Lime Bavarian Cream sliding from his hand. She took it from his hand, put it on the crowded bedside table and went to stroll the hall while Phil slept. Maybe there was a window somewhere.

As she roamed the hall, a doctor stopped her, a young resident working the ward, a nervous young man.

"Can I speak to you about your father?"

"Sure."

"Has he had—uh—emotional problems before? He has been causing some trouble on the ward."

"Trouble?"

"Well, he threw a pop bottle at a nurse. And yesterday, yesterday, his roommate's wife came in to see her husband and he wasn't in the bed. Your father told her he had died."

"He's always been, uh, difficult," Jane said carefully, amazed at her own use of euphemism.

"We can't handle that here. There's a psychiatrist coming to see him to-morrow. We believe he's suffering from depression."

Good thinking, Jane bit the words. "I'll try and talk to him." She had a sense they wanted to be rid of him, to kick the misbehaving patient off the ward. They were not in the least amused.

"Phil—Phil, what did you do to the nurse?"

"She's a bitch."

"Phil, you can't throw things at people. I won't bring any more 7-Up if you're going to throw it at people." She was sure he was living on 7-Up. Each time she came in he asked for it, ice cold. And she served it the way

94

he had taught her to make ice-cold water when he came home from the office, ice in first.

Jane didn't mention the other incident, as the man was in his bed.

"Phil, there's a psychiatrist coming to see you tomorrow."

Phil looked away.

Jane softened her tone. "You don't want to get moved to a psych ward, do you?" Threatening whisper. Behave, mister.

"Is Owen coming today?"

"I don't know. When did you last see him?"

"Maybe this morning."

"I'll phone him when I get home."

"Where's Gene?"

"In Toronto. He went back to university. He'll be back at the end of term."

"How about a little chopped liver?"

"I'll phone Ruth when I get home."

"She was here today, Ruthie. Brought me 7-Up."

After Phil eased back to sleep, Jane looked in the cupboard beside the bed. A bag of oranges.

On the way home, Jane pulled Phil's car into the parking lot of the tiny hotel beside the bridge. An old rural hotel, a reminder that this was once the main street of a separate town. She stopped to buy beer.

Smelled the clear cold in the air.

Snow falling.

November.

Later that month Jane phoned Sophia for her birthday.

"I have news," Sophia said, "a letter from Ireland. Your cousin Evan has a daughter. Her name is Rosa."

"That's nice. Is Uncle Charles pleased?"

"Well, I would think so, only it's the strangest thing." Sophia lowered her voice. Conspiracy.

"What is?"

"She was born on the day Maeve died." Superstition.

"But that's good, Soph."

"Well, I suppose so . . . What makes you say that?"

"Just there's something to celebrate, then. Changes the day."

" . . . I guess you're right." Sophia sounded temporarily relieved. "Still, of all the days in the year," she added hauntingly.

Sophia tried not to be obvious about her superstitions. Once, when Jane was young, Sophia came home from a luncheon wearing a beaded jacket inside out.

"Your jacket's inside out."

"Oh. Well, I'm so short-sighted."

"Didn't you feel the beads?"

"It's bad luck to change a shirt that you put on inside out."

"You left it on purpose?"

"Oh, no, I just didn't notice."

On New Year's Eve, just after midnight, Sophia sent a dark-haired person out the back door of the house and around to the front.

"It's bad luck for a year if a red-head comes through the door first."

"Says who?" Gene asked.

"We always did it at Home," Sophia said.

"At Home" meant Ireland.

Eire.

The Irish Republic.

Sophia left home at twenty. Went to London. To escape.

"Escape what?" Jane asked.

"Home. Family. Ireland."

"What did you do there?"

"I worked in a hotel on Russell Square, night desk clerk." Sophia smiled, gazed into history. "I went to the theatre. Gielgud, Olivier, Ralph Richardson, Wendy Hiller. What an actress. My shift started at four in the afternoon, and went until midnight. I went to matinees. If you waited until the play was about to start, you could get a seat in the stalls at reduced prices. And I'd sleep in late. The chef would make me fried tomatoes on toast for breakfast in the afternoon. If they wouldn't give me holidays when I wanted to go to Paris, I'd just quit and go. And I'd get my job back when I returned. You could buy books in Paris."

"English books? Why buy them in France?"

"France is a civilized country. You could buy books there that were banned in England. They'd sell them with brown paper covers with fake French titles. I smuggled *Lady Chatterley's Lover* in that way. At the customs they always had two lines. One for British subjects, one for everybody else. I'd go in the one for everybody else. Then I'd get to the front and show them my Irish passport. 'You're in the wrong queue,' they'd say. 'I am not,' I'd answer, 'I'm a citizen of Eire, the Irish Republic.'"

"And then they'd let you through?"

"Oh, no. They'd send me to the back of the other line. But I still did it every time." Sophia laughed.

"What was it like when you came here?"

"What was what like?"

"The city."

"Well, I'd hardly call it a city. It didn't look like much after London. You couldn't even get a drink in a restaurant. We had to take wine in, in a paper bag." Sophia looked disgusted. "We lived with Baba and Zeda at first, then we rented our own place, when Owen was born." Sophia was quiet, memories running black-and-white film of an era too harsh to forget.

"What was that like?" Jane watching Sophia's eyes, straining to see what they saw.

"Pardon me?"

"What was it like living with Baba and Zeda?"

Sophia studied Jane. "Your Baba was very kind to me," she said after a decision. "It was very different from home."

When Owen and Jane wheeled Phil into the little house that he had bought from his hospital bed, his eyes looked with relief at the variation of the walls. The fireplace and mantlepiece, the familiar paintings, his plants on the wide oak window sill drew his attention out into the world beyond his mind.

"The magic is back," he announced quietly. "I'm lucid. I'd like to invent a way of doing blood analysis without needles. Maybe lasers." Bundled in sweaters and blankets, his head barely rose above the back of the wheelchair. Gene and Owen slid their hands under his thin thighs, and lifted him gently onto the couch. Jane transferred the tube and bag for his urine.

Phil was home. Two months after the surgery.

Home for a day.

Jane awkwardly hefts three bags of groceries onto the kitchen counter. Gene ate everything there was to be eaten, then flagged down the bus back to Toronto out on the Trans-Canada highway. Before he left Gene ran into Colin, whom they had known since childhood. Colin, who lived here year-round, who recognized a Gene he hadn't seen for ten years because of his striking resemblance to Phil.

"I told myself it couldn't be," he said smiling, "then I realized."

"I know, I know. So how are ya?"

Gene arranged for Colin to come by with his truck and haul away the cut caragana, but he hasn't shown up yet. One of these days.

"It's getting quiet now," Jane sings as she fills the refrigerator. She folds the bag carefully and puts it in a drawer, "sometimes it just will." She opens a cupboard and lines cans up on the shelves, remembers stripping labels off all the cans when she was a child. To make a fort. It looked better when all the cans were the same colour. More like building blocks. For months Sophia opened cans randomly and the children ate whatever was inside.

"It seems we got no right," she folds the last bag, "to be so still." The cabin feels empty without Gene. She wanders out back, sits on a half-rotted log. The old chopping block. Hunts in the woodshed for the axe.

Jane rests a dead tree she has already dragged down against a large rock. Raises the axe above her head. Swings it down.

"Have you got shoes on, dear?" It's Sophia. "No chopping without shoes on, Jane."

And her own young voice answers teasingly, "I won't miss, Mom."

Even in memory, Sophia shudders.

The axe cracks down on the deadfall, Jane's hand sliding the length of the handle as it falls, increasing the weight.

Crack.

The dry wood snaps in two, more from the force than the sharpness. The old axe is hammer-dull.

Jane shifts the log. Braces it with her foot.

Raise and

crack.

Wood for the fire, company for tonight.

Crackle and burn. Dance spirit. Bring back the ghosts.

Hands behind your back. One, two, three.

As the children play it, paper covers rock.

Snip.

IV

EVOLUTION

Love as piercing as the screwdriver's thrust.
Love as searing as the marks on an infant's leg.
Love as clear as her face.
Love as clean as a sheet of yellow paper.
Love as honest as a poem.

BETH BRANT
Telling

History is collective memory.
Remembering is a process of cracking stone.

July. Summer sun calls fire from the earth.

"Forty-seven forest fires are currently burning," says the voice of the radio announcer, as Jane mixes tuna and mayonnaise, pours orange juice into a glass filled with ice. She unfolds the *Muddy Water Free Press*, reads reports of fires to the north and northeast of the park that contains her meteorite lake. Fires have never threatened here, though Jane has seen the air thick with smoke blown in on a prevailing wind. Her three-year-old eyes itched as smoke wafted across the Trans-Canada forty miles west. Phil driving carefully between fields of smouldering ash. The slow re-growth to a low forest, watched over the years during the hundred-mile drive between here and Muddy Water. She has driven herself through the charred moonscape stretching ten miles east of Kenora, grey rocks, upright greyed tree bones. Mile after mile, and that only the small area where the fire leapt the highway blowing southwest.

There are summers like this, every seven or eight years, summers that burn and burn. Water bombers rush overhead. Too little snow, too little rain. From spring thaw to summer drought. Jack pines calling fire to seed them, trees that will only seed in scorching temperatures. There must be fire. July calling fire from the earth.

Outside the dry is quiet. Though some afternoons there is no break in the whine of water bombers overhead, Jane does not worry as one engine fades and another arrives. If it didn't happen in the past, it won't happen now. There is no present beyond investigation, beyond excavation, beyond the brothers who have come and gone, beyond the woman, Marie, who might be waiting, waiting yet, even though she is out there in the world where the phone is always ringing and someone is always interested.

The caragana is moving. Has moved. A landscape slowly shifting tenses. Childhood hills rise on either side of the cabin. Climb smooth surface lava. Look down. Sophia at the cabin door. Thin and lanky, zipped into her white terry-cloth jump suit. Sunglasses, hair held off her face in a hairband. Her split stomach muscles protruding slightly. Little pot belly. White shimmers, breeze rustles dry branches. Ghostgone. Jane stares down from the rocky crag.

In 1918, Edith and Max were married by Rabbi Meyer Bernstein, on a quiet February Sunday in a dry winter that ran to sheet ice and hoar-frost mornings. Edith stood in the small living room of her parents' house, facing her future with the same steady confidence that had dreamed, planned, and executed every stitch in the satin and lace dress gracing her light skin. She knew every stitch was in place, in the right place, invisible. She knew her mind was as clear and as sharp as that of the man who stood beside her, and if she was a little less prone to blow in a prevailing wind, that could hardly bring ill upon them. She knew her life, her children's lives, could be dreamed and planned and executed as expertly as her dress. It was a matter of mind and will, of education and application to the task at hand, of respect for yourself and others, to achieve a valued place in the community. "*Mazel tov!*" The muffled sound of glass breaking in cloth brought Edith out of her reverie. She turned to face everyone and gave a slight nod, before walking to the couch on which her ailing father lay. As she knelt to receive his blessing, he said, "If you would only know how glad I am to have lived to see this day."

"And many more," answered Edith.

"And many more," he repeated quietly. That was Edith. She did not give up. "He is a good man," said Peretz Rice, who had seen men of Ukraine, of Rumania, of Germany, and those of many countries who had travelled to this new land, where a man from elsewhere might pretend he was anyone. "He's a good man, Edith, *mazel tov*," he repeated, for he knew that all his daughter needed in a husband was a man who was good to his word. The rest she could do herself. And for all the doubts that he harboured about young Max's roaming, for all the rumours of his flashpoint temper and fighting in the street, it seemed to Peretz that this Max had pride. Pride would make him match Edith's mettle. Pride would make him husband to his wife. "*Mazel tov,* Edith," he patted her hand gently, "and now, I should rest a little bit."

Over the years, when her children asked, Edith told them how she and

104

their father had a large, festive wedding, with plenty of food and dancing and *mazel tov*s. It wasn't until after she died, when a cousin visited Muddy Water from New York City, that they learned how Edith and Max had married at her parents' house, so her father, who was dying, could be present. A small family wedding, at home.

Three decades later, Max had a stroke that left him hemiplegic. Though he couldn't speak, he managed to curse his frustration. He was cared for at home by his wife, Edith, for six years, three months and eighteen days. In Jane's family photo album there is a picture of him, a thin grey-haired man with large eyes peering out of a sombre madness, lying on a couch, surrounded by a wedding party. The occasion is the wedding of his son Josh—Phil's only sibling and twelve years his junior—to Aunt Ruth. The picture was taken in the living room of Max and Edith's house, the house with the large white peonies in the front yard.

Stone heaped on stone becomes a foundation.
History repeats itself.
Father to son becomes father to son.
A foundation of forgetting.
A pattern of stone.
Evolution never repeats a pattern.
The earth beneath your feet moves up and down a foot each day, every day.
The earth beneath your feet spins round and round itself.
Round and round the sun.
Erodes, heaves, buckles, hardens, softens, blows away, dust in a some-time wind.
Ashes.
In a sometime wind.

"History shouldn't be taught," Sophia told Jane, in the small house by the Atlantic.
"Why?"
"That's how hatred passes on. That's how history repeats itself."
"But we wouldn't know about so many things, things we can learn from," Jane argued.
"It's just hatred. They teach you to hate someone for what their father did to your father. Just wipe the slate clean, I say, start from point zero today."

"But I've met young Germans who are furious that they were never taught anything about the concentration camps in school."

"And what did it make them feel?"

"Angry."

"You see my point."

"I don't. They were angry about what they hadn't been taught, they didn't want to hate anyone, they just didn't want to be taught denials."

"Exactly. So, history shouldn't be taught. If it isn't hatred, it's denial. All they would have learned is why some people hated them, and then they would have opportunity to return that hatred."

"Or offer redress, or at least understand redress, or totalitarian monstrosity."

"That's philosophy," said Sophia. "You can teach morals without teaching history."

"But you used to tell me all sorts of history in your anecdotes and stories."

"Women get more radical with age," said Sophia. "The teaching of history is the preaching of hatred."

"And what about love? How can you teach that?" Jane asked.

"By actions," Sophia said quietly. "Don't you remember?"

Phil begged not to be sent back to the hospital.

"I want to stay at home."

"We'll have you back as soon as we can, Phil," Jane heard her own condescending tone and cringed.

"It's my house and I want to stay." Owen hovered in the doorway.

Jane wrapped the blanket around his withered body and tucked it under his bandaged foot.

"We promise," Owen added, "we'll have you back home as soon as we can."

After Owen and Gene left with Phil, Jane collapsed on the couch. Numb. Her body pressed into the soft upholstery by the weight Phil had shed, by the dressings on his bedsores, the diapers that received his incontinence, the cruelty of the bone that protruded from his stump. She was exhausted by his requests for special dishes that he could not eat for the ache in his stomach, by the fear in his eyes each time their untrained hands tended his fragile body, by her knowledge that she could not do this day by day.

Gene went back to Toronto.

A few days later, Owen phoned Jane.

106

"They want to meet with us."

"Who does?"

"The doctors."

"Why?"

"They want to send Phil home."

"You're kidding."

"No. Why?"

"He's too sick."

"He wants to come home for his birthday."

"We can't do it Owen. I can't do it. It's not adequate care."

"Phil wants to come home. Come to the meeting."

Jane went to the meeting. Explained that Phil wasn't getting adequate care at home. He didn't eat. There was no dressing on his stump. The dressings on his bedsores needed changing. He couldn't transfer in or out of the wheelchair by himself, which meant he didn't use the toilet.

"If you don't want to do it, I will," said Owen.

"Have you got another sister?" Jane heard a doctor ask Owen as they left the meeting.

Two days after Christmas, Owen brought Phil to his house. The room was filled with relatives, wishing Phil a happy birthday. Eyes avoiding eyes. Phil on the couch in a sweater and blanket. Cold, always cold. Energy slowly draining from Owen's face as he insisted on doing everything to take care of Phil.

You didn't want to. Each action said it.

"I'm a dirty old man," Phil said suddenly, his eyes loose with tears. As if on a signal, everyone moved to the far end of the room. Jane sat beside him. Took his hand. "I pooped." He was crying.

"I'll do it," said Owen.

He was crying.

They cleared the room.

"I'll do it," Jane offered quietly.

"No." You   didn't   want   to.

Jane went with Owen to drive Phil back to the hospital.

"Please don't let me get cold. Please don't leave me here."

Owen sat in the car as she wheeled Phil in.

Stroked his hair.

"You can leave him here," said the nurse at the station. "We're just changing his room."

"Don't leave me here   Jane   Jane   Jane." The words trailing after her down the long quiet hall.

"Did you have a good Christmas?" Jane heard the nurse ask.
"I'm Jewish," Phil snarled.

A man out of time.

The dry caragana snaps easily in the clippers, heat thwarts the mosquitoes and draws Jane's thoughts toward the water. She cuts low to the
ground, re-clearing quickly toward the tall oldest growth. Eight- and
nine-foot caragana, as thick as her wrist, lean over the rock crest above.
Today she will try them, at least until the heat wins. The caw of crows in
the background reminds her of June, of the ground still cool in spots, still
damp. Long weeks of heat and sun have warmed and dried the land.
Leaves rustle beneath her feet, crumble to dust.
High above the cabin, she cuts. Arms strengthened by weeks of work,
saw moving through stems. Controlled pressure. The sound of the blade
on wood. The crack of the stem breaking. Tosses it down, on top of the
low growth she has just re-cut. Waiting for rain. Rain to loosen the thin
soil so that she can pull roots. To dampen fires burning out and beyond.
To moisten these crisp dry days of July.
Cuts. Tosses. Clears a space in her mind. How sunlight reached the top of
this hill, how the long grass grew here, brushed against her knees.
Brushes against her knees. Jane looks down. Sees a small brown bear
just beyond the pile of cut caragana below the hill. Remembers one huge
bear, five feet long, lumbering down to the water as Sophia hurried Gene
and her along the path to the far side of the bay, climbing up with the
wind behind them. Watching the bear wade into water, roll out onto its
back, wide and slow, heavy, lolling in the lake, stretching legs too thick
to stretch, lumbering through the water, each movement starting a wake.
Gigantic as it waded out and wandered up into the hills.
But this is a cub. Loping from side to side. Long limbs, skinny body. As
soon as she sees it, it's gone. Where's the mother, Jane wonders.
Sophia's rule: Don't worry unless you get between a cub and its mother.
A thousand hokey nature shows on television celebrating the mother's
instinctive protection of the child. Animal or human. Instinct like a hom-
ing device, special radar. You cannot prevent yourself from following it.
Automaton definitions of motherhood, fatherhood.
You cannot prevent.
Jane succumbs to heat and Sophia's wisdom, takes off her gloves as she
walks down the hill. Thinks about canoeing over for beer.
In the cabin she turns on the radio at the end of an interview with a

woman who trains horses without ever beating them. Lucky horses. Jane slips into a bathing suit, picks up some shorts and a towel.

News follows the interview. "In Toronto today, a Superior Court judge refused to give a man an injunction to prevent his former girlfriend from having an abortion. Lawyers for the Canadian Abortion Rights Action League claimed the decision as a victory for all women."

As her feet pad down the old path to the water, Jane thinks about men seeking injunctions to prevent women from having abortions. Floating on her back, a wide blue sky quiets the rocks that rattle inside her. The image of a large bear lolling. Water erodes stone, wears it smooth as cold skin. Wonders what a court would do if a man sought an injunction to stop a woman from working. Say the woman was pregnant and working and the man argued that her job might cause a miscarriage. Sees, in clear water, how civil rights, for men and for women, have different definitions.

Jane mops her skin and slips on her shorts. Canoe into water, paddle, push off. Glide, silent, floating. Quiet motion. Moving soundlessly. Beaver, nose at the water line. A ripple on the surface. Silence and grace, a beaver in a northern lake. Water is second nature. Like breathing in and breathing out.

Silent and graceful like a beaver on a northern lake. Float. Peaceful. At peace. Rocks quiet. Weightless, drifting, not home but free. This body, this sky, adrift.

"All I want is a nice cold beer," Jane sings, to a tune from *My Fair Lady,* one of Sophia's songs of longing. Then she laughs. And laughs. She is here and now. Weightless and drifting in slow-motion freedom. And laughs.

Six months after Phil died, Jane went to the ocean to visit Sophia for a weekend.

Sunday morning, Jane moved restlessly around the small house.

"You're just like your father," Sophia snapped suddenly.

"I am not."

"You can't even sit still and relax. Just like him."

"Why bring him up? He's dead. Forget it."

"I can't forget twenty-five years with that man. That bastard."

"He's dead already. Can't you see?"

"You treat me just like he did. Like a stupid child."

"I do not."

"Twenty-five years of being treated like a child. Manipulated, screamed at," Sophia slipped into history, "humiliated. Oh, the times he humiliated me." Weeping.

Jane watched twenty-five years of fear live on past the agent. Wished for a grave that she could take Sophia to, and say, here, look, see the name here. Feel this cold stone. Listen, hear the silence of the wind. He is buried in this ground. There is peace. He is no more.

And he can't hurt you.

But he still could.

It took Sophia seven years after leaving Phil to unlearn the fear. She spent two years fearing him after he had died.

Then had two happy years, before she died overnight.

In Sophia's obituary, Jane asked for donations to a shelter for battered women.

In a changing society, those seeking strength from new sources foster and nurture their own institutions.

Granny crocheted and knitted. Baba Edith sewed. In 1968, the year Martin Luther King was shot, the year Robert Kennedy was shot, the year Pierre Trudeau was elected Prime Minister, Granny crocheted Sophia a daring white cotton skirt and jacket, see-through. Baba Edith sewed Sophia a grey satin pantsuit.

Sophia began to think about running for the legislature.

She chose between three ridings, all held by the government, but all considered possible to change.

Won the nomination for her party in one of them a year later.

The first candidate to declare.

The election call came suddenly. They always do, even when expected.

As the campaign progressed, Sophia became more and more optimistic. Candidates always do. It's the only way to have enough energy for the task.

Calculating that Sophia would draw votes in the burgeoning tide of second-wave feminism, the other two parties both nominated women. Or maybe she just opened a door.

On election day Jane and Gene sat in a church auditorium, carefully drawing a line through the name of each voter that filled in a ballot.

Owen and Phil were out pulling the vote.

The poll clerk Jane sat with, a retired army veteran, looked over at Gene slumped in a chair reading a book, his face hidden by hair he was reluctant to comb.

"What that fella needs is a few years in the army," the poll clerk said.

"That'd clean him up."

He's not dirty, Jane thought. She was twelve. Then she thought, I'll never be Sophia.

Sophia would have said it.

In the midst of a shocking victory for her party, Sophia lost.

The men who ran for her party, in the seats Sophia didn't choose, won.

When they got home after midnight, Sophia sat down in the living room, with the lights off and began to weep. Jane sat on the staircase, watching Sophia's reflection in the mirror as she talked with workers from her campaign and cried and talked some more. As they strategized and hypothesized about the new government. As they consoled. At three in the morning, Jane went to bed.

When Jane woke up at seven, Sophia was still sitting in the living room, her eyes red and running, talking quietly with a bearded young worker about the new era. 1969.

Sophia loved politics. It was a passion that moved her from thought to speech to action, that made her heart quicken, the blood rush a little more fully through her veins.

A new era was dawning. This provincial government wasn't led by an Anglo-Canadian. The cabinet was made up of men who traced their families back to the north end of the city. Men whose names were German and Ukrainian and French and Jewish and Polish. Men who appointed Sophia to positions of power. First, to the film censorship board, where she refused to censor any films, denounced censorship and resigned. Then to chair the Social Assistance Appeal Board.

Men, who had the power to appoint her. Men, on whom Sophia was dependent for her access to power in government.

Muddy water and it moves so slow.

But at least it had begun flowing.

Sophia itched to make it move faster, yearned to have her hands deep in the flow, urging the trickle to a rush, and the rush to a flood.

A passionate compassionate flow.

Jane could see it in her eyes. Learned there, in Sophia's eyes, how to love a thought and an act, a way of being. A woman in direct contact with the larger world. Unmediated.

The course that Sophia longed to re-direct was that of history.

In the making.

After the birthday at Owen's, Jane and Gene spent his vacation time rearranging the little house to accommodate Phil. The surgeon was determined to discharge him. The door came off the tiny bathroom next to Phil's bedroom, a curtain went up in its stead. The king-size mahogany bed was dismantled and stored in the basement. Drawers were cleared for dressings, diapers and needles for insulin injection. Doses of insulin, nitroglycerin and pain killers were stockpiled in the fridge and cupboards. Sixteen-hour-a-day nursing was scheduled, and an orderly to visit once a day to bathe Phil and transfer him to a chair. Jane filled the refrigerator with cran-apple juice, which Phil now drank steadily, and asked friends for recipes for smooth, easily digestible foods, thinking of Lime Bavarian Cream. On the second night after Gene returned to university, Jane sat with Phil as he rested in the large green leather reclining chair. The house was quiet. His wounds were dressed. The night nurse, duties done, was watching television in the living room. Phil was calm and relaxed. There was the kind of fragile peace that a moment of equilibrium brings in a sea of tension. The precious fleeting peace when an infant ceases crying and drifts to sleep, when a death pauses in its slow progress and lets a dying man live for a moment.

"Remember, Janey," Phil said quietly, "remember the sunrise at the lake?" A blaze of crimson across the black silhouette of the treeline on the far shore.

"Mmm-hmm."

"And how calm the water is on a hot morning?"

"Calm as glass, Phil, calm as glass." He smiled. It was his phrase.

"That's right. Calm as glass. You wouldn't think it could kill you, when it's calm like that."

"No, Phil, you wouldn't. But that lake would never kill me."

"Oh, you can swim alright, Janey, you can swim like a fish. But anyone can drown, even a good swimmer."

"But not a fish. Fish don't drown."

"No, fish don't drown." He laughed. "You gotta catch them."

"How come you never learned to swim, Phil?"

"When I was a kid we didn't have lessons, you know, we just went to the beach, took the train to the beach, the boardwalk and all that, it was so shallow that—" Phil's back arched. His head flipped back. His eyes rolled up under his eyelids. Jane stared as Phil's mouth sprang wide and his tongue flopped out at her. Up and running for the nurse Jane noticed Phil's foot flinch as the arc of madness peaked. By the time she was back with the slow-footed nurse he was twitching, gently. Jane took his hand. The nurse went directly to the telephone.

"What   happened?" Phil whispered. Far away.

"I don't know, Phil. Just rest, now, ok?"

His eyes closed slowly.

Jane let the ambulance go into the hard January night without her. She followed to the hospital later, the car awkward and stiff on frozen tires. Decades below zero.

Grand mal seizure, they said. And Jane remembered the epileptic seizure of a high school classmate, how he shivered on the linoleum sheen.

Don't know why it happened, they said.

Can't say.

Don't know if it might happen again.

Or not.

Phil remained in the Hospital of the Holy Martyr with its crucifixes and nursing sisters as the cold clear skies of January exacted winter's brutal price from the residents of Muddy Water. Jane gradually felt her body remember what it was like to live in Muddy Water, how to feel the freshness of the cold and ignore the bite, how to discern the warmth of the pale white sun as her cheeks reddened toward freezing, how to enjoy the shimmering of light on the snowbanks without thinking about the accompanying temperature. She remembered to pull the drapes closed as the light began to fail in the late afternoon, remembered to turn her attention into the house, refusing to acknowledge the long hours of night. By February, Jane was no longer slowly remembering how to endure winter in Muddy Water, she was living inside her knowledge of twenty winter years. She was waiting, with the rest of Muddy Water, for winter to stretch beyond their endurance.

Then spring could come.

Early in February the phone rang in the house in which Phil never lived. "The hospital called, they want us to go to a meeting, Thursday. I can't make it. Can you go?" Owen asked.

"Sure, what's it about?"

"Not sure, the social worker called. Here's her number."

"I have it."

Jane hadn't spoken to Roberta Harris, the hospital social worker, since before Phil's first visit home. Once the hospital bed and attendant equipment had been delivered, once the nursing and orderly support had been arranged, Jane hadn't heard from her. Roberta Harris explained that the hospital wanted to move Phil to the extended care unit, where he might be more comfortable, but before they could do that, the family had to meet with the head doctor and staff from the unit. Some members of the unit were sceptical about the move.

The streets were thick with snow and sand as Jane eased the car along the wide main boulevard where she had spent Saturdays downtown shopping with her friends. When the Bank of Canada had hiked interest rates a hideous six per cent overnight the previous November, Muddy Water businesses dropped like flies in a sudden frost. The frozen economy was visible throughout the downtown shopping district. Jane drove past store after store emptied of stock, idle "For Rent" signs caught her peripheral vision as she rolled along toward the bridge across the crisp white Muddy River and on to the hospital.

Sceptical.

The meeting was in a small conference room. Around a hospital-clean veneer table sat the doctor in charge of the unit, the head nurse, two staff nurses, an occupational therapist, a physiotherapist, Roberta Harris, and Phil, in a wheelchair, with an orderly beside him.

As Jane sat down they introduced themselves to her, and to Phil.

"Do you know me, Dr. Cammen?" asked the occupational therapist, who had just introduced herself as Ellen.

"Would I be right if I said you have something to do with cones?" Phil responded. Ellen laughed gently.

"That's right, we work with cones in occupational therapy."

Dr. Wilson introduced himself and the others, and explained that an extended care unit did not treat patients aggressively in an attempt to cure. "We try to enhance the quality of life. We usually only accept elderly patients who are not very ill. Dr. Cammen is younger and more ill than our usual patients. We don't have as high a ratio of staff to patients."

"You can't go ringing for a nurse all night," a staff nurse named Sharon interrupted him. A sceptic revealed.

Phil nodded obediently, like a child chastised.

"Do you think you'd like to move to this unit, Dr. Cammen?" asked Dr. Wilson.

Phil looked at the nurse Sharon. "Yes," he said quietly. "I think it's for the best."

Dr. Wilson nodded, and the orderly rose quickly. "I'll take you back to bed now, Doc."

As the door shut behind them, Dr. Wilson said, "There's one more thing. Because we aren't trying to cure patients here, we usually ask for a non-resuscitation order." The room was silent. Jane was suddenly very small and very young, trying to understand why the room and the people in it had become so large. Why everything seemed to be turning upside down, whether it was the whole world that had inverted or just this one space in it. Why the top of the table she was sitting at was brown and so shiny that she could see her own blank face in it. How these strangers could be pressing up against her so tightly and yet be so far away that words wouldn't reach them. Why she had never asked god to shake her curtains.

It was only when Dr. Wilson said "Perhaps we'll leave that for now, then," that Jane realized she had left them all in silence while she stared dumbly at the question that had been asked. She looked at no one as she gathered her coat and scarf and ran her hand along the rough wool of the coat, just to feel it.

Her first complete thought occurred long after she arrived back in the little house.

"I just never expected it," she said to Shulamit over the phone to Toronto. "I mean, he was always such a tyrant, I just couldn't believe someone was asking me whether or not he should be revived."

"What did you say?"

"Nothing, nothing at all. I was too stunned. It was very embarrassing for everyone."

The routine medical decision fused with the immense personal decision as soon as Dr. Wilson's words reached Jane. All the years of her family history, all the words Phil had knitted into her bones, all the boxes and controls and roles, told her she did not have the right to make this decision.

But they had asked her to.

And she had befuddled everyone by thinking about all of it, before answering.

For days Jane tried to find an answer for Dr. Wilson. Trying to cross the distance to the answer, unconsciously aware that her failure to answer was an answer that meant the question would have to be asked again.

"The next time this happens," Jane caught herself thinking, "I'll know exactly what I'm doing."

It's a long way between love and hate.

And no distance at all.

Some years after Phil's death, Jane came to the conclusion that they should have asked Phil. But by then, she knew, so much of that year had already turned to stone.

At the end of July, Jane stands behind the cabin, sipping a beer and looking for the past. The piles of cut caragana are blocking her view. She will have to find Colin soon. See if he will bring the truck down for a load or two. She sees what looks like a bank of grey clouds coming in from the west, goes into the cabin and turns on the radio, listening for rumours of rain. Sits down in an armchair, her feet on logs she has piled on the hearth.

"The Aboriginal Justice Inquiry has been declared invalid by the provincial Court of Appeal. The Court ruled today that the challenge to the tribunal brought by the Muddy Water Police Association is valid, in view of an earlier ruling by the Supreme Court of Canada that all provincial laws must be drafted in both English and French. The order-in-council creating the Inquiry was drafted only in English."

"Ah, shit," says Jane, "that's a lawyer for you. Since when did the Police Association give a good goddamn about drafting laws in French?" Jane thinks about the bigotry and hatred aroused in the province when the government of the day, in anticipation of the Supreme Court ruling, tried to make the laws bilingual. Of the opposition leader who whipped prejudice to hysteria, producing hate mail and bomb threats and then riding a crest of vicious popularity out of politics and onto the benches of justice. "Where else for such a man?" Jane mutters, wondering if he made the ruling himself. "I wouldn't put it past the little bastard," she says, then realizes she's sitting in Phil's favourite chair, cursing the same people he did.

Even as she laughs, she knows, as does the Francophone community and every other community in the province, that the Police Association had no interest in French language rights and every interest in seeing the Inquiry derailed before it undertook to examine the circumstances of the death of J. J. Harper, an employee of the Island Lake Tribal Council, on the streets of Muddy Water, of wounds caused by a bullet fired from a police revolver. And the circumstances of the police investigation into the event, which initially cleared the officer whose revolver was fired, within thirty-six hours. Jane feels the rhythm again, the pull of evidence. The rush of detection. A mystery. She stands, and paces, as if addressing a jury.

Sometime between March 1988 and July 1989, it became clear to the Muddy Water Police Association that their members could be held accountable for their actions by another duly constituted legal authority. So they set out to undermine it. She turns as thunder cracks heavily above her, momentarily blurring the radio. Then the voice crackles through again, "The government immediately re-constituted the legality of the Inquiry with a bilingual order-in-council." Jane smiles. But, she says to the jury in her mind, they arrived too late. The Inquiry already had an existence which sustained it beyond legal invalidation. Moral authority granted it by all those who had come forward to speak, by all those who followed its activities in newspapers, on television and on radio, by all those whose inclination toward justice had been awakened by its promise. There are people, all over the world, who do not like it when the forces of law and order shoot unarmed citizens, Jane muses. There are spirits at work, ready to testify.

As the announcer begins the weather report, Jane hears water pour from the grey clouds which have settled in low around the cabin. Looks out on rain in sheets thick across the water. Rain for miles. Drumming on the roof, drenching the trees, running rivulets beside the cabin down toward the lake.

Jane starts crumpling newspapers to lay a fire, stops to read an article in the national paper about the Inquiry. Halfway through it reports that a joke had circulated in the Muddy Water Police Department.

"How do you wink at an Indian?" the joke goes.

Then a hand mimics the barrel and trigger of a gun.

And the thumb fires.

She rolls the paper into a ball and lays it on the grate. Stacks kindling, lays on split logs, from an old poplar she has chopped. Strikes a wooden match and sets it to blazing. Dances. Spirited.

Growing up in Ireland fostered in Sophia the belief that the teaching of history was the preaching of hatred. The lessons of history as Granny taught them.

"Your Granny supported the Provos until her death," Uncle Charles told Jane when she visited Dublin after Sophia had died. Granny died in 1980. "Times had changed," he said smiling, "but not your Granny. Granny believed in the Provos."

"That's where your mother studied botany," Charles said, as he drove Jane past a large and distant greenhouse.

"I scheduled my classes so I could sleep in late and go to all the balls," Sophia had told Jane, many times. Jane pictured a young Sophia in a floor-length gown out of *My Fair Lady*, riding off to a high-society event in a horse-drawn carriage to the tune of *I Could Have Danced All Night*, though Sophia much preferred the longing of Eliza as she sang about the comfort of a warm room with a coal fire and an enormous chair. Sophia was inclined toward songs about escape to a place that offered calm. And she considered *My Fair Lady* a bastardization of *Pygmalion*.

"In *Pygmalion* she doesn't marry the professor. Don't you see? She says she's going off with Johnny. They missed Shaw's point entirely. A complete bastardization."

"How come you can say bastardization but you can't say bastard?" Jane asked.

"Bastardization is a perfectly acceptable word," Sophia answered. Case closed. Too bad for the professor. No more ball gowns or fur wraps or tiaras, no more catering to a bully who condescends to your intellect and humanity.

The trade Sophia was longing to make.

Phil always said that when he first met Sophia she was reading *The Intelligent Woman's Guide to Socialism, Capitalism, Sovietism and Fascism.* G. B. S. Sophia called him *Bernard* Shaw.

Sophia told Jane she met Phil at a party in London.

Said she was married in a registry office.

Wearing a navy blue suit.

A response to Jane's grade-school inquiry. The other girls talked about their mothers' weddings and wedding dresses.

A navy blue suit, Jane discovered, was not the expected thing. She said it with the same proud air Sophia had given it.

A Navy Blue Suit.

Fact is a matter of fact.

It was a relief for Jane to know there wasn't an aging white lace dress up in the cedar closet, waiting for her to grow into and reanimate it. A long-discarded Navy Blue Suit created no obligations.

A Navy Blue Suit was from somewhere else.

And none of Jane's young classmates could picture a registry office in London, England.

It was all too modern for the neighbourhood of the Citizens' Committee. Too casual.

Just like their household.

Too idiosyncratic.

Like their family.

The form was cracking.

History, like a navy blue suit, was going astray.

In jeopardy of not being repeated, and of evolution.

The morning after the rain, Jane goes back to the top of the hill. Stumps and roots of old growth. She has an axe, a shovel and a small gardening fork. Hands.

She shoves the fork under a stump. Hefts a boot onto it. The stump lifts, barely. Tendrils pop like swollen veins, map the lifeline of caragana. The journey back. Fingers into damp soil along the roots, roll gently. Pull, roll gently, pull, along along along. Musty, rich earth. So close. Pull roots free. Free. Six feet from the stump, loose from the ground.

Back to the stump. Crouch, lift, four more tendrils spring a web from the ground. Along each, shovel under, up, shovel under, up. Careful, along, along, along.

Back to the stump. Shovel under, kick, lift. A giant spider rises from the ground. Hands on the stump, raise it high. Toss it down.

Jane slumps to a crouch. Closes her eyes and sees his. Phil's. Those long, dread-filled months. Mind a lingering disease, death slowly becoming a metaphor for freedom. The only way out.

"It would have been easier," Jane says, eyeing another stump, grinding earth in her hands, "it would have been easier if I had been his wife. It would have been easier to say 'Let him go. He's had enough.' If I had ever experienced the world without him in it, or if I was his age, or if I could have seen that his suffering was greater than his desire to live."

But that was just it, he wanted to live.

He wouldn't let go.

She could see it in his eyes.

While Reb Haskell Cammen and brave Reva were being legislated out of farming and into tenancy as keepers of the inn, the British were carefully imposing their hated rule on the land that wanted to be known as Eire. British landlords forced Irish tenants off the land for failing to meet exorbitant rents, or simply because the lord wanted it clear of tenants. Kathleen Barry lit peat under cauldrons of water when word came, through the ladies of the Land League, that police and bailiffs were afoot. She listened quietly as troops built a battering ram, praying to the saints that the peat would burn quickly, that the water would rise to boiling, before the sides of the cottage began to quiver and shake with the unholy pounding of the men who did the devil's work. *Hail Mary fullofgrace theLord iswiththee.* But the saints were estranged from Eire in those days, the British pact with the devil held strong. *Blessed artthou amongstwomen.* The pots of half-heated water that Kathleen and her mother flung at the marauders were no match for the Imperial army. *Andblessedis thefruitofthywomb.*

The echo of shattering walls resounded as the family stood fast on the land, holding to the tenancy as long as they could, hoping the sisters Parnell of the Land League would put an end to this theft. They had followed the Land League's advice, refusing to pay the usurious rents, supporting the strategy that would soon become known as the "boycott" after Captain Boycott, collector of rents for the British, to whom the strategy had first been applied. The echo resounded as they called upon relatives already resettled in Londonderry. Relatives already settled in neighbourhoods whose names would become famous in the 1960s and '70s, as those Catholic enclaves struggled on against hated British rule. *Holy Mary Motheragod Pray for ussinners now.*

Kathleen Barry joined the legion of women who worked in the mills in the north and longed for the freedom of Ireland. She married there and wept with her husband at the fall of Parnell, all the while standing by the clergy that damned him. Kathleen Barry saw to it that her daughters were schooled in the image of the good ladies of the Land League, that they grew up into the struggle for the Irish Free and Catholic State, straight-backed, well-read and well-versed in the crimes of the English. For love of the country, for love of their mother, the Barry daughters would rise up for the Irish Free State.

And at thehourofour death.

For their hatred of the British, who had thrown their parents from the land, the daughters, Grace and Patricia, would fight for the Irish Free State.

Amen.

One of those daughters was the woman Jane came to call Granny.

Love and hate are opposites.

Opposites repel sometimes.

Sometimes they attract and bind in a common cause.

The sea oh the sea is the *gradh geal mo croide*

Long may it stay between England and me

It's a sure guarantee that some hour we'll be free

Thank God we're surrounded by water.

The emerald isle.

When Sophia's Uncle Owen, who enjoyed escorting her to balls and parties in her botanical years, died, Granny sent Sophia his collection of Irish records. An old orange hand-stitched plastic cover arrived in the mail to the house with the fossilized fish in the limestone front. It held twenty-three singles, songs by the Dubliners, the Travelling People and others—*Kevin Barry, Nelson's Farewell, Dublin in the Green*; a history of rebellions, hangings and bombings, some mourned and some celebrated—the songs of Ireland. Among the music was a skit Jane and her brothers listened to repeatedly. Two old women, a Catholic from the south and a Protestant from the north, are riding the bus from Belfast to Dublin. The bus crashes just as the two are getting into a heated argument.

"If someone drew a line round my neck, it wouldn't separate my head from my body," says Mrs. Macalhagar of Ulster.

"Of course not," answers old Mrs. Mulligan. "If someone put a rope round it, now that would be different."

When they arrive at the pearly gates, only the Catholic, Mrs. Mulligan, is offered wings. The Protestant Macalhagar is told to take a "long slide down." When the guardian of the gates cannot be persuaded to hand over a "coupla secondhand crowns," Mrs. Mulligan refuses hers. "They've put a border between us on earth," she says, "but we'll sink or swim together now." Macalhagar weeps and the clerk of the gates finally relents. "Ireland united. No politics. No bigotry. No fighting," declares Mrs. Mulligan.

"No surrender," adds Mrs. Macalhagar.

Lying on the carpet in the big living room Jane listened to the spinning 45 over and over, waiting for the line, "Put on your wings Mrs. Mac, and we'll have a spin as far as purgatory and back." Sophia had explained that Catholics believed in heaven, hell, purgatory and limbo. As an un-baptized baby, Jane, said Sophia, would go to limbo. But Jane believed that, in such a scheme, she was surely headed for purgatory. Purgatory called to her mind the suspension of religion in her family and life, in general, in the quiet city sprawled amid the echoing expanse of winter prairie. The waiting.

After the February meeting, Phil was transferred to a single room in the extended care unit of Holy Martyr. The ward was calmer and brighter than any of the wards where Phil had been previously. Phil was more comfortable and more lost. Occasionally a voice drifted down the hall, yelling "B-16" or "O-52," another patient randomly reliving the weekly bingo game as he rested in a chair in the hall, his expensive track shoes hanging idly over the edge of the chair.

Jane sat and read Phil the newspaper, or the latest book by one of Canada's chroniclers of history through caricature and anecdote. Often he drifted to sleep as she read and woke startled to find her sitting there.

"What year is it?" he asked.

"1982."

"What month is it?"

"February."

"What day is it?"

"Tuesday."

"What date is it?"

"The twenty-third."

"Where am I?"

"Holy Martyr hospital, extended care unit."

Phil's thick eyebrows scowled. Suspicion. Could be trying to kill him.

"There's someone under the bed."

"There's no one under the bed."

"There's someone under the bed. Look. It's that big guy, the one who makes me sit in the chair."

"Phil, the orderly is not under your bed."

"Look, damn it. Just look."

"Ok," Jane bent, "I'm looking. There is no one under the bed."

"Must've left before you came."

Other times Phil would already be sleeping when she arrived, and Jane would sit and read, knowing he would wake before long.

"What year is it?"

"1982."

"Month."

"March."

"Day?"

"It's Saturday, March 6, 1982. This is the extended care unit of the Holy Martyr hospital."

"Are my parents dead?" he asked suddenly, staring into the years between the bed and the wall.

"Yes," Jane answered, and watched Phil watching their images dissipate.

"Why did I take a job at the Veterans' Hospital in 1947?"

"I don't know, Phil. Why did you?"

"Best orthopaedics section in the city. I was a G.P., just back from the war. I was thinking about orthopaedics—even though it wasn't a residency it was the best place to be in Muddy Water. Then I got a call from Victor Holmes, top orthopod in those days, said they were setting up a clinic, and he wanted me to join."

"And did you?"

"Not then. I'd made a commitment to the hospital, and I didn't have any capital. But I began to work with Victor and he really got me started. Then, I decided to go over to England and specialize, and join the clinic when I got back. 'You'll know more than we do by then,' Victor told me." Phil stopped. "Read to me, Janey. What's happening in the world? Where's Owen?"

"Busy, really busy."

"Where's Gene?"

"In Toronto. He'll be back next month, after exams. Then we'll be able to have you home more often."

"Who's the Abbott?"

"The Abbott?"

"See, he's there. Up on the wall. A little man. He comes to see me. He makes arrangements."

"Phil?" Jane looked toward the place where Phil's eyes fixed on the wall, a lighter spot in the shape of a cross, where the crucifix must usually have hung. The hospital staff had taken note of Phil's Jewishness after he started ordering kosher meals. He told Jane the food was better on the kosher menu, told the same to the rabbi who visited briefly after Phil changed his meal choices. Phil preferred the kindly and soft-spoken visiting sister who made no effort to talk to him about religion.

"He's a little fat man," Phil was saying. Jane silently pictured a benign Buddha figure hovering cross-legged on the wall. Radiant and smiling innocuously.

"Phil—who is the Abbott?" Jane asked pointedly. Uncomfortably.

Phil eyed her cautiously. "Read to me," he said.

And she did, until he drifted to sleep.

Sophia's political career culminated in her appointment as chairwoman of the Social Assistance Appeal Board. For the most part, she drew little public attention. Day by day, her work was to visit the home communities of appellants. Her rulings and orders for increased payments of social assistance usually mattered only to those involved. Gradually, however, they began to catch the attention of the reeves and mayors of the local municipalities who were required, by law, to carry out Sophia's dispensation. Required to pay a little more out of the municipal coffers.

Then Sophia was invited to address the annual meeting of officials of the province's municipalities. Feeling the smooth sure wood of the gavel in her hand, Sophia told the duly elected rulers of the province's fiefdoms that the amounts of money they paid to families on social assistance served only to "bring a family from the level of total starvation to below subsistence level." Citing statistics that indicated one rural government paid only ten dollars a month for food, Sophia did not equivocate. "I do not believe," she announced, a trace of Ireland faint on her low voice, "that we should be guilty of this slow, cruel program of deprivation—this genocide. I use the ugly word genocide very seriously and after much thought. I do not use it lightly. I believe it is imperative," Sophia challenged the collection of car salesmen and general store owners, of lawyers, Rotarians and at least one descendent of the Citizens' Committee of One Thousand, "to apply to the poor the same code of rules as we do to others within our community. I believe that the intention of your organization to create lists of those on municipal and provincial assistance is both regressive and reactionary; anonymity is possibly the only protection the poor have. I see with deep regret that this is another form of intimidation of an already intimidated group."

In spite of the hope Sophia expressed in closing, that the officials join with the provincial government to ensure full development of all citizens in the province, "without violation of or jeopardy to their values, dignity, or their freedom of choice," the cat was already out of Sophia's bag. The shit, as Phil was later to say, had hit the proverbial fan.

It was Sophia's forty-eighth birthday. Saturday, November 13, 1971. The afternoon that became the evening that became the long long north November night.

The Muddy Water papers ran page three stories with headlines that highlighted the word "genocide." "APPOINTEE ACCUSES ELECTED OFFICIALS OF GENOCIDE" read one, which also carried a long editorial deriding socialists from wealthy neighbourhoods who advocated doling out, with largesse, the hard-earned tax dollars of the province's citizens and dubbed Sophia "Lady Bountiful." Her party was vilified as "a collection soft-hearted strangers to economic reality." The second paper, being somewhat more progressive, ran a flattering photograph of Sophia, with a caption that read "Cammen gives genocide speech."

Genocide entered the family vocabulary.

"What is genocide exactly?" Jane asked Sophia.

"The deliberate destruction of a people," Sophia answered, stirring a can of cream of tomato soup into a bot of parboiled milk.

"By starvation? You should put the soup in first then heat them together."

"By any method. Why?"

"Then it won't get lumps. Like the Jews in World War II?"

"That's one example. It always has lumps, that's just the way it is."

"I'll do it. Who else?"

"The Beothuk in Newfoundland."

"Yeck, it's all lumpy. Who else?"

"It won't hurt you. All of the Indigenous peoples of the Caribbean islands."

"Tastes barfy. Who else?"

"Just eat it. This is depressing. Genocide has happened throughout history."

"Why would anybody do that?"

"Hatred," said Sophia, setting bowls on the table, "deep-seated hatred, failure to recognize the basic rights of every human."

"Hatred."

"Uh-huh."

Jane looked it up in the dictionary. Genocide: extermination of a race.

Slow, cruel deprivation.

Subsistence social assistance, segregated communities, hostile employers, the closed door of bigoted landlords, the sharp dividing line in movie theatres that guarded "white" seats. Sophia called that genocide.

Assimilation or death.

On the long long north November night.

Jane postpones finding Colin. Instead, she gradually moves the piles to a single one beside the woodshed, out of her line of sight. The past again becomes more visible in the present. As she lifts and carries, she hears Sophia's voice running like a stream in a rainfall. Sophia calling her children in for supper, Sophia explaining why plates must be cleared from the table, why beds must be made and wood must be chopped, why caragana must be cut. Why certain words should not be said and others are entirely appropriate, why dragonflies shouldn't be caught and trapped in jars, why Baba Edith doesn't serve butter with roast potatoes, why they should never go swimming alone. Why profits should be taxed and medical care, housing, clothing, food and education provided at a level at which all citizens can live, whether they can work or not, whether they can find work or not. Why caterpillars turn into butterflies, why Ireland was two nations, why the value of a society should be measured in how it treats its weakest and meekest.

Measured in caring.

Voices. Water in the rain. Hugging the ground, running quick and light. Sophia here with them, summer after summer. Through bears and storms and power failures. Sophia gone. Suddenly. Permanently. Like childhood. And all that she took with her. Longing like a warm empty place you have to get used to. She is there and not there, that is the problem, the essence of longing for something in particular, for someone, dead and alive. The ways you will find and not find. Memory, where overgrowth can be cleared away.

In a philosophy of emotion, feelings are accorded the same importance as facts.
Neither is devalued, because it's not a question of one or the other.
In school, Jane and her brothers were taught that *man* is distinct from other animals because of his ability to reason.
Binary logic.
Yes. No.
Either or does not make a story. Either the protagonist lives or she dies, either she loves her parents or she hates them, either she misses them or she's reconciled to their deaths. Either her parents should have married or they shouldn't have. So, the story must either be about death or about life, not about death and life, death in life. About history and the future, hatred and love, a person and a family. About pain and about healing. About events that happened and events invented. Memory waking in a churning mind.
Paper and scissors and rock.
Paper covers rock, scissors cut paper, rock smashes scissors, paper covers rock.
Hands behind your back. Fists closed. One   two   three
Either Sophia was much happier as soon as she left Phil, or she succumbed to the patterns of mind that had developed in the years of their marriage and was afraid, humiliated and bitter, wishing she had left sooner. Or, she realized that she had left, and Phil had died and she had her life and her Bob and her modest comfortable house overlooking the ocean. Innisfree. And that was enough to have, until the next time memory intruded on her sanctuary.

After moving the piles, Jane swims, loosening her cramped arms, easing them through small waves that curve across the surface of the lake. She dries herself slowly, enjoying the breeze slipping over her skin. She strips off her bathing suit and lets the wind dance gently on her body. Open and calm. Wraps the towel around her hair and walks up the rocky path to the cabin, opens a beer and turns on the radio, to listen to the world beyond.
The news reports that the re-constituted Inquiry has just heard the testimony of James Houghton, one of the two men tried for the murder of Helen Betty Osborne. Houghton, says the reporter, has told the nation

via television, the night before his scheduled testimony to the Inquiry, that he was not present at the deserted pumping house on the long long north November night. As Jane dries her hair with a towel, they air a tape of Houghton being questioned at the Inquiry.

"You are not telling me that you were not there?"

Silence.

Jane pauses, blood cold. She does not want him here, even his silent voice.

"Do you have any recollection of that event?"

"No recollection. As far as I remember, I wasn't there."

"Were you not there or do you have no recollection?"

"No recollection."

"So you're not telling me now that you weren't there?"

"No."

Jane stands, towel in hand. She is cold. Murderous cold.

His memory is a stone wall.

A good detective knows when someone is lying. Jane walks outside and pulls a sweatshirt off the clothesline she has made with a rope between trees. She can still hear the radio. "Following his testimony, Inquiry Justice . . . " the screen door slams, drowning out the voice, " . . . told Mr. Houghton, 'You're either a very stupid man or you're a liar. And frankly, we think you're very intelligent.' " The reporter goes on to quote James Houghton as saying, "I sleep well," when asked, and Helen Betty Osborne's mother as calling him a liar, in Cree.

After his testimony, the reporter says, James Houghton went home. To resume his life, as if nothing had happened, Jane having read earlier that home is no longer the small town in the northwest of the province, divided by the Saskatchewan River into the white town and the Cree community, the town where felling and processing trees into lumber and paper remains the major industry. Where the movie theatre is no longer divided into a "white" section and an "Indian" section, where bikers still roam the streets on HarleyDavidsons after the bars close, but full-blown street fights between white bikers and Cree and Métis youths no longer disrupt the long twilights of summer just north of the fifty-fourth parallel. Where members of the white community now work for Cree-owned businesses in the attractive mall built by the Swampy Cree Tribal Council on their side of the river, built after the failure of a lawsuit to stop it brought by white merchants.

Jane muses, as her stomach rumbles for lunch, that probably this very minute, at the sawmill, and in the planer mill too, two lunchrooms are filling with the sons of The Pas. In each mill, one room will be filled with Cree and the other with anglicized Europeans.

Evidence.

Might be any town from here to Vancouver.

Detection requires concentrated imagination. Jane tries to imagine a man who would fit the voice of James Houghton. She imagines it is evening. He has travelled home, unflinching. He is lying down, in a twin bed. Far away. He is closing his eyes and sleeping stone sleep. Even though it is summer, there is a chill in the room. Cold stone.

In 1905 Reva and Reb Haskell Cammen arrived on the Canadian prairie with their three children Max, Miriam and Zalmen. By foot, by boat, by rail and by wagon they had come, by hook and by crook and by the good graces of the minister of immigration, who had been tentatively convinced that Jews, though known to be inveterate traders and moneylenders, could farm. The government needed farmers to clear and break the land they claimed for the Crown, broad grassland no longer free to be roamed by bison or the peoples it had spawned. Land that would be fenced and tilled and broken, land that would be forced to yield for the good of the nation, as had its inhabitants. The Jewish gentry of Montreal, in collaboration with international Jewish benefactors, had lobbied the federal government, providing guarantees of supervision and loans and farming education, until the government conceded that it might be possible for Jews to cultivate land. Soon every Jewish man immigrating to Canada knew that he had to declare himself a farmer to the inspecting immigration official.

Reb Haskell, born on a farm, twenty years an innkeeper and collector of rents, state-enforced stranger to the tilling of land, stood before the small, sickly-looking immigration officer on the docks outside Quebec City, said "Farmer," coughed loudly and clearly with no trace of congestion, and entered life in a new country. With relief the family boarded the train for the west, glad to escape the overcrowding of the dockside warehouses, assured that when they finally arrived, they would be greeted in Yiddish and transported out to the colony. Reva rested her tired body against Haskell, scooped a child in each arm and drifted to sleep to the rocking sound of steel on steel, the rails of the great Canadian railway. They had travelled from Vinitza to Kiev, from Kiev through Poland and Germany, as she had dreamed, her precious family, her life's blood, arriving in Bremen. Reva cajoling the children when they tired, "*Nu, Maxala*, a long way to go yet, we're crossing half the whole world." Waiting anxiously through nights on the Bremen wharf, rolling with the heave of the Atlantic, doling out *matzos* and dried beef as they waited for the sea to end, waited for their feet to feel again the firm soil of the earth. And finally, onto the train, and no one had the influenza that leapt wildfire through the immigrants' warehouse on the St. Lawrence dockside, none of her children are hot or complaining of pains in the stomach, no one is coughing or spitting, and they are almost, almost there. On the wheels roll and Reva dreams on, believing she has been sleeping and waking for three nights and days, and still when she wakes Haskell says, "No, not yet."

Then finally, Haskell's voice, drifting across the Ukrainian plain, drifting clearly into her dream, "Reva, keep your eyes closed."

"Haskell?"

"Trust me. Eyes closed, Reva," he said in Yiddish. "Imagine nowhere," his voice said quietly, and Reva's mind opened into a broad empty grey. "Nowhere with snow and snow and snow," below the grey, white, endless white. "The sky is blue, Reva, the sun is shining, Reva, and everywhere, in every direction is snow and sky." Above the white, endless blue, and the sun searing along the surface of the snow, open and cold in Reva's mind.

"And the land, Haskell, where is the land?"

"Reva, I'm sorry, the land is the snow and the snow is the land."

"Haskell, surely it's spring now?" Reva asked, not wanting to open her eyes and see what was already so clear in her mind.

"Reva, God forbid this is spring if we're trying to be farmers."

"Oh, Haskell." Reva opened her eyes on the razor line that separated the blinding white snow from the sharp blue sky. "Haskell, it's beautiful." Reva shifted a son to wipe her watering eyes.

"Beautiful, Reva?" said Haskell. "It's the middle of nowhere, frozen solid."

"Haskell," Reva cut in, "we're safe, the children are healthy, and there's space, room to breathe, like, like," she hesitated to use the word home, "like Vinitza. No more warehouses, no more sleeping with strangers like so much cattle. We'll have a home and fresh air and spring will come and the sun will shine on all of us."

"All that may be so," Haskell answered, "but what is a Jew without his community?"

They lasted one winter in the young Jewish farming community at Lipton, Saskatchewan. One winter in a mud dugout, with future promises of a log cabin to be built by the community. Reva tending the children, Haskell exhausted after a summer spent building the dugout, felling trees

129

and carting rocks to clear the land, trying to make ready for spring planting, wondering how he would make payments on his low-interest loan
from the Jewish Colonization Association, wondering how his children
would be educated in a village that had no school and only a temporary
shul of sod and rock, wondering if winter here was a test intended to
pierce the bones and sharpen the soul, wondering if he should have
stayed in Muddy Water where there were roads and stores and formal
schooling and a proper synagogue under construction. When the first
breath of spring slipped over the crust of snow, when birds could be seen
overhead and the silence of the wind was broken by their singing, Reb
Haskell Cammen took one last look at the rocks slowly protruding
through the melting snow, and made his decision.

"A Jew must have a community," he announced to Reva's back as she
bent over a pot of slowly warming water in which she would wash the
children's outermost garments.

This will be a community, she thought, but said nothing.

"But for now it is only a scratch and a prayer," Haskell answered her
thought. "At the first opportunity I'm taking our prayers to Muddy Water, and we'll scratch there, where things are already started."

And so Max and Miriam and Zalmen were moved to the north side of the
great Canadian railway tracks that divided Muddy Water into Anglophone and non-Anglophone communities, on the west side of the
Muddy River. In the heart of a growing Jewish community Max began
the schooling that would give him the "unaccented Muddy Water English" that would get him a job at the Muddy Water Electric Railway
Company twelve years later, his sister Miriam began to play with the boy
who would grow into the chill-hearted man that would drive her into a
mental hospital to escape her marriage, and the youngest, Zalmen,
would hear of the land called California, where fruit grew on trees and
snow never fell, to which he would immigrate with his young wife and
wait the rest of his life to be joined by his big brother Max, whose departure was planned and delayed and planned and delayed and finally cancelled, first because his wife Edith's father was dying and then because
her widowed mother was too sick to cope on her own, and Edith would
have them stay to care for those who had cared for her.

As spring teased Muddy Water, Jane felt a surge of relief and a wave of
foreboding. She never let more than one day go by without making a
visit to the hospital, to see Phil. She read, thought, stared out the window, wrote letters to Sophia and to Shulamit, bought good Italian

espresso and spiced olives, German sausages and kasha knishes and waited. Something would happen. Gene would return soon, they would bring Phil home on rotating visits as soon as there were enough hands to cook for him, feed him, bathe him, change his dressings, change his diapers, transfer him to a chair, wash the laundry and fold proper hospital corners to prevent further bedsores. Soon, but not yet.

Jane drove through streets made dusty by the sand the city government dropped in the winter to provide traction on ice and snow. The trees were bare, a slow parade of ice was drifting down the Muddy River. Spring was the ebb of winter, not yet renewal.

Phil's manic eyes met Jane's as she entered his room.

"Hi." She tried to sound bright. Engaging.

"Hi." He eyed her dubiously.

As Jane placed her bag of 7-Up and kiwi fruit on the chair he said suddenly, "What would you say if I told you I had a cheque for three million dollars under my left elbow?"

"I'd ask you how you got it."

"The Abbott gave it to me."

"Why?"

"Royalties. He's arranged it so I get royalties every time that show's played—you know, the one about the radio station."

"TV show?"

"Yeah. *CKRP* in Cincinatti, you know."

"WKRP."

"Yeah."

"Why would you get money every time that show is aired?"

"It's a scam. The Abbott arranged it."

Jane looked over and saw the little Buddha-figure hovering placidly over the shadow of the crucifix. Get the hell out of here, you little pest. She aimed the thought at his radiant smile. He wavered and then vanished.

"If you've got the cheque, let's see it." Phil made no move. "Come on, Phil, lift up your elbow."

"Can't."

"Why not?"

"I don't have it."

"Where is it?"

"At the bank. You don't think I'd keep three million dollars in a hospital room, do you? I thought you were supposed to be smart."

"Thank you. How did this cheque get to the bank?"

"Bank manager picked it up this morning."

"Phil."

"You don't believe me, call the bank."

"I can't call the bank, there's no phone in here."

"Ask at the nurses' station, they'll give you one."

"No."

"You don't believe me and you won't even find out if it's true. I'm a sick old man and you won't even phone a bank for me." Phil glared and Jane tensed, stuck between will and delusion.

"I'll do it myself, if you won't," Phil snarled and rang for the nurse.

"Never mind," Jane growled back, wanting the delusion to end, yet not wanting to live the moment when it crumbled.

When she came back with the phone and plugged it in, Phil immediately ordered her to dial.

"I don't know the number."

"Phone information. Main branch, Bank of Montreal." She dialed and wrote down the number given to her.

"Dial," he said again.

"No." Jane handed Phil the paper.

"Alright, goddammit, I'll do it myself. Here I am dying and you won't even make a phone call for me."

"Phil, there is no cheque. Why would the bank manager come to the hospital?"

"Can't even make a simple phone call for me." He began to dial. Jane watched, hoping he would misdial and give up.

"Hello," said Phil, and Jane turned to stare out the window. Her eye caught the glowing figure of the Abbott cross-legged in the corner of the room. A corner of her mind. I thought I told you to get the hell out of here.

"Yes," said Phil. "This is Dr. Phil Cammen, I'd like to talk to the manager."

Silence. The Abbott gleeful.

"Well, he's, he's, he's got a . . . " Jane heard a pause and the sound of the receiver replaced in the cradle. Pop. The Abbott was gone again.

Without looking at Phil she walked over, unplugged the phone and left the room. At the nurses' station she handed it to the head nurse, whose mother had been a schoolmate of Phil's. Phil praised her constantly, calling her by her mother's name.

"Are you ok?" she asked Jane.

"I will be in a minute." Jane closed her eyes and struggled to relax without succumbing to sadness. "My father has these delusions," she explained, looking at the woman.

"It's common, you know, isolation, illness, incapacity."

"Yeah, I guess so. I mean, I can understand why, he's quite literally bored out of his mind. I just don't know how to deal with them."

"Ask him detailed questions."

"Well, there's this guy, the Abbott."

"Ask him what he looks like, how they met, detail."

"Thanks. But I don't think I can do it."

"Maybe someone else then."

"Yes, sure," Jane felt a bit lighter, "someone else. Thanks, thanks a lot." She'd tell Gene. Gene would do it when he came home. Goodbye Abbott.

That evening, Jane phoned Owen and told him the events of the day. Later that week, Owen mentioned that he had watched *WKRP*, to see the credits. "Just in case, you never know."

"You know," said Jane, "you're no help at all. You're crazier than he is." Owen shrugged, smiling.

If *man* is only distinguishable from other animals by virtue of his ability to reason, what is he when emotion overcomes that ability?

Dying slow.

Roll on Muddy Water, roll away.

Roll away the year that laid a man so low.

August. Motionless. Calm. A still, sunny summer day, gentle undulation of clear water against shoreline. Summer feet. Hardened to the stones, moss, needles, roots. Knowing this familiar ground. Toe to heel. To head. Footwork from cabin to water's edge. Right, left, rock, root, root, left, right, left, right, grass, root, root, jump, rock, rock, dock.

Liquid against skin. Body buoyant, safe. Breasts, face airwarm, legs, back watercool. Ache seizes water soothes rocks into sand. Relieves the tension of research into relentlessness.

Summer air, gentle around, quiet as day ends. Summer feet water to cabin. Dock, jump, rock, rock, sand, left, right, root, root, grass, right, left, root, root, rock, stairs. Turn, beauty stares you down. In the eye of the beholder. As evening falls, as daylight eases away, as the first star glimmers faintly in Beardsley blue, as the northern lights begin to flicker on a cooling August evening.

Summer holding, bones sense autumn settling in to wait. A hint in the night air, a warning on the surface of the water in the morning. Warning: cut   listen   remember.

Keep the rocks moving.

Or they'll settle again.

As she sips scotch and gazes on the lake, Jane listens to an in-depth radio report on the Aboriginal Justice Inquiry, which has just heard the much-awaited testimony of Dwayne Archie Johnston. Her hands drum on the window ledge. Her eyes roam the water. This is the man. The only man convicted of any crime in connection with the abduction, assault, sexual assault, forcible confinement and murder of Helen Betty Osborne. The one whose loss of freedom must somehow compensate for the long long north November night, the night echoing across the second-largest country in the world. Loud and clear, Jane thinks, just tell us loud and clear. The reporter says Mr. Johnston was brought in from the Saskatchewan penitentiary where he lives under armed guard. He took a seat in front of the two Inquiry justices, and with his mother watching, he refused to swear an oath.

"One hundred and fifty people gathered at the hearing," says the reporter, "most of them Métis people and Cree people, heard Dwayne Archie Johnston announce, 'There's been a lot of things said and I could talk for five days and nothing's gonna change.' And watched him leave."

Jane swallows a long pull of scotch, stunned. He refused to say anything about the long long north November night. "Lips sealed tighter than a dead man's," Jane snarls.

The reporter is saying something about Johnston refusing to speak, "unless he is moved into a court of law."

"I really do believe he is innocent," says an older woman's trembling voice. His mother speaking to Jane over the radio. Instinct.

"GUILTY!" Jane shouts. Pounds a fist on the window sill. "Guilty, guilty, guilty, guilty. All of you. Did and done, boys," she says, thinking not just of Dwayne Archie Johnston and Lee Scott Colgan and Norman Manger and stoney James Houghton, but of the Johns and Jacks and Daves and Toms she went to high school with. The ones who used to go down to the legislative grounds where gay men cruised. Let themselves get cruised, invited up for a drink. Drink, beat the man up, and leave. Bashers. Who would break someone's jaw for speaking to their girlfriend. Bashers whose grandfathers were the government's hired goons in the General Strike.

"Guilty, guilty, guilty, guilty."

It could just as easily have been them, Jane knows. If the residential school by the bridge hadn't been closed by the time they could drive, it would have been. As a teenager she avoided them, as an adult, she'd like to go back and turn them in to someone for every vile act they committed. Make it stick on them for life. She knows this Inquiry isn't about two killings, where and how they took place. It's about a country and its history. Our history.

When the report ends, a light entertainment show begins. Jane turns off the radio as Madonna begins to sing about a material world, and steps out into new darkness. Trees shading green to night. Bat shadows overhead. Idle star, wishing softly *star light* moon hovering *star bright* burgeoning *first star I see tonight* breeze rustles water poplars *wish I may, wish I might* woman's voice distant *have this wish* Sophia calling *I wish tonight* Marie loving past and present confusing. Jane slides into dreaming, sitting on the steps, gentle in the darkness of the night.

Baba Edith sewed every item of clothing her children wore until each was in their mid-teens. She produced school clothes, play clothes, starched white shirts and wool jackets for synagogue, fashionable dresses with curt waists and billowing sleeves leading to elegant collars. She gathered and pleated, hemmed and overstitched, pumped the pedal on her trusted straight-sew, slipped the needle seamlessly through chiffon and seersucker and homespun and gabardine, and occasionally through a fine piece of silk purchased at a well-bargained price on Selkirk Avenue. Baba Edith rolled strudel dough as thin as tissue paper, fine cabbage leaves from Max's garden around carefully spiced mince for cabbage rolls, rolled yeast dough with cinnamon, brown sugar and raisins into cinnamon buns, rolled almond cookies through powdered sugar before she set them on a plate for Max to have with his tea.

Baba Edith worked.

Sewed and cooked, baked and prayed, washed and planned for the future. The future was her children and her children's children, and after that, "God willing, I'll be dead." Baba Edith translated for new arrivals, Jews who kept getting off the train in Muddy Water all through the twenties, arriving with husbands and children, with parents and siblings. And very little else.

Young Edith translated when they negotiated for jobs and for housing, when their children came down with fevers and influenzas that all of their nurturing skills could not cure. Edith translated from Yiddish to English and English to Yiddish, Russian and Rumanian. When she was asked to interpret in a court case involving the disappearance of three chickens from the yard of a recent arrival, and the reappearance of what appeared to be the same three chickens a few blocks further north, she provided her services, but refused the payment offered.

"My husband has a good job," she told the clerk of the court, thinking of how he had recently turned down a promotion to supervisor. The money was better, but the Depression had begun, and as a supervisor he had less security. No union.

Better to stay on the rails.

"You turned it down?" said Max, when Edith explained. "So, their money isn't money?"

"You want they should think you couldn't support us?"

"No. But you could've bought yourself a new dress, a nice hat."

"I can make any dress I want, and my sister makes hats the best in the city."

"*Nu,* a little fabric then."

"I work, in this house," said Edith firmly. "Outside this house, I do, because I'm interested. For the community."

"My wife, she's just like a south-end lady," said Max, "she's doing her charity work."

Edith fixed him with a calm eye. "And why not? Are they any better than us?"

"As God is my witness," Max said solemnly, "you are the finest of women, Edith. As God is my witness."

Unruffled, Edith slid the pin from her hat and went to put on her house shift. The smell of roasting chicken permeated the small house. There were candles to be lit, prayers to be said, bread to be broken and shared. It was *Shabot,* and Edith was the equal of any woman, south end or north.

Our children will be proof of that, she thought, buttoning her dress.

And our children's children.

And then, God willing, my work will be done and I will go to my rest.

But not, it turned out, before she lived in the south end herself.

Though there had been Jewish families in the neighbourhood of the Citizens' Committee of One Thousand since shortly after the time of the Committee, it was not until after the Second World War that Jewish families began to be numerous in the Muddy Water bastion of Anglophones and Anglophiles, Anglicans and Free Masons. The neighbourhood expanded rapidly south. Trees were levelled, land was cleared and one-storey box houses with picture windows and stucco siding were built side by side by side. Detached. There was space on the prairie. A neighbourhood laid out on an even grid, a development, built before the era of instant developments. The south end of the south end, where Phil was able to help Max and Edith to move after Max's stroke. To the bungalow, with the picture window on the front and hearty white peonies that blossomed in the unrelenting summer sun.

By then there was a small, square, simple synagogue built in the neighbourhood, that Baba Edith could walk to on a Saturday morning, pushing a mute and angry Max along the few treeless blocks. In the bungalow, Edith Rice Cammen nursed and tended Max and his frustration through the last of his life, nursed and tended for the last time someone who was terminally ill. Her Max.

History is a process of collective memory.
What gets forgotten is lost, edited from history. Until someone goes digging.

Through the waves of humanity seeking freedom and peace and prosperity at and after the turn of the century, Muddy Water grew and prospered. Until the doors of the country slammed shut in the tunnel of the Great Depression. The city buzzed again in the fifties and sixties, hummed with the new life of the post-war generation, hummed with the new life of births and arrivals, of progress and prosperity, and then slowly ceased. Muddy Water settled into a comfortable size, settled into its uncomfortable patterns, settled into seventies inflation and eighties depression, barely avoiding Yuppies and liberalism, but succumbing to racquet clubs, malls and video cassette recorders.

The neighbourhood of the Citizens' Committee retained its status as the apex of wealth and prestige, of snobbery and insularity well into the sixties. Then, as newness overtook tradition in the economic boom years, the neighbourhood itself became a stepping stone to a flashier area with swimming pools and tennis courts, named after a man's dress suit. But, within the neighbourhood of the Citizens' Committee the old hierarchy ruled. Those who moved on to swimming pools, tennis courts and golf clubs were viewed as upstarts who cared more for flash than for grace and tradition. The other rules were simple. As the neighbourhood expanded to the south, away from the river, gradations of status were developed. The closer you lived to the river, the better. For those who paid heed to such things, each block closer to the Muddy River was a step closer to substance, each move toward it signalled a step up in the ranks of the tiny society that cared. Of course, there were those who just lived there. Those who chose the neighbourhood for the canopy of elms and oaks over the roadways from spring to fall, who preferred the quiet that permeated the streets, who liked to stroll the broad avenue that paralleled the river on a Sunday. But sooner or later they discovered someone around them who was counting the blocks to the river. In that, Muddy Water was not unusual. It happens everywhere. It just sits harder in a place that's five hundred miles from another city, it sits harder in a city whose children leave to discover the world out there, a city that has been disregarded by the machinery of economic growth, that sits sedately on the panel of prairie, no longer even waiting for another chance to flourish. Waiting only for spring to follow winter, and summer to burst, brief and brilliant, from the hardy seeds of spring.

Winter is long along the frozen Muddy River.

As the last of the ice melted into the river, Jane drove through April rain to the hospital. How well she now knew this little bridge that slipped from the backside of the warehouse district to the main street of the old Francophone town. Past the burnt and resurrected cathedral, past the residences of the Catholic nursing order that had established the Hospital of the Holy Martyr with its orange neon cross glowing strangely in overcast skies. God'll be hard pressed to see through to us today, Jane thought, amusing herself. "Clouds so swift, rain won't lift, gate won't close, railings froze" she sang quietly as she walked slowly down the hall to Phil's room, past the man yelling bingo numbers from his reclining chair, past the woman who had asked Jane for a kiss after seeing her kiss Phil goodbye, past the nurses' station, where she was called over.

"We think your father has salmonella," said an older staff woman Jane recognized but did not know by name.

"Salmonella poisoning?"

"Yes."

"How would he get that?"

"It may have transferred somehow from his feces."

"Feces?"

"You know ... "

"I know what it means."

"Sometimes his hands," the nurse began, but was stopped by Jane's grimace, "anyway, we'd like you to wear a pair of latex gloves if you're going to be touching him. And we'd like you to go to your doctor and be tested."

"For salmonella?"

"Yes. You do have a doctor, don't you? Because if it's not convenient, we could arrange to have it done."

"No, thank you, I'll do it," Jane promised, backing away toward Phil's room.

Get your mind off a wintertime, 'cause you ain't goin' nowhere.

"Phil. Hi. You're up."

"What's that noise outside?"

"Thunder. There's lightning too, like a summer storm. Summer's coming, Phil."

"Summer? How long have I been in here?"

"A long time. Too long. Gene'll be home soon and then we can bring you to the house sometimes. You can stay there for a while, and then here for a while. But you'll always be coming back home."

"Is that Big Bertha outside the window?"

"Who's Big Bertha?"

"Not who, what. Big Bertha's a gun the Germans have. Part of the fortifications on the French coast. But we should be south of there."

Jane stared out the window at rain sluicing down the length of a murderous steel barrel. Into the grey and the rain. Sophia's voice came to her, "No formal religion," explaining to a ten-year-old Jane what to write in the space for religion on a school form. "Put 'NFR,' for no formal religion, or, if you're sure that you don't believe in god, put 'agnostic,'" Sophia had said.

"How do you spell that?" Jane asked.

"A-g-n-o-s-t-i-c."

"NFR is easier to remember."

"Yes, it is."

"But I think I'm ag—agnostic."

"Really?" Sophia asked.

God was an old man. Old men were scary. "Yes." Sophia gave Jane a tell-me-more look, but Jane said nothing.

"No, Phil, I don't think it's Big Bertha," Jane said gently, returning from reverie. "I think it's just thunder. Why did you join the army, Phil?"

"To fight Hitler. I was ROTC—Reserve Officers' Training Corps—which meant they paid me monthly, supplementing my savings and my scholarship. Your Uncle Simon joined and suggested I do. Then he finished law and I finished medicine and we both joined up. Commissioned officers right away. I made captain before I was demobbed."

"What did you do in the war?"

"I sewed people up. Had a mobile unit just behind the lines on D-day. Went in on D-day, Janey."

"It was penicillin that saved them," he said after a pause. "Antibiotics.

139

We'd never seen anything like it. A cure. It was like magic. Before that most of them survived the wounds, but they couldn't withstand the infection that set in. Died like flies. Then, suddenly, a miracle. Never saw anything like it in forty years of medicine. A bloody miracle. Healed clean every time." He drifted to sleep, woke. "Jane, hold my hand," he said, and dozed again.

Jane left the window, pulled a chair to his bedside. He woke again as she was pulling on a latex glove she had taken from the drawer in his night table. "What's that for?" he asked.

"Salmon—" she started to explain, "oh, never mind. Nothing." She pulled the glove off and threw it in the garbage. She slipped her fingers between his, felt the knuckles of the surgeon's surgeon's dying hands, and willed her strength to flow to him.

A scary old man.

Christmas in Muddy Water was a family engagement. Christmas as celebrated by Phil and Sophia was food and gift-giving and a pine tree decorated quietly after arguments, acrimony and stormy departures in the process of getting the tree to stand in the house. It had nothing to do with Christ or Christianity or church, and everything to do with family. By the time Jane visited her Irish relatives for Christmas, she was twelve and had never seen a mass celebrated. She had been in church once, for a wedding. Jane had been in synagogues many times, for weddings and bar mitzvahs. The Christmas Jane looked forward to was waking early and opening presents with her brothers, while Sophia, dozing on the couch, woke, shared their pleasure and drifted back to sleep. Later there would be a large breakfast cooked by Phil, *Miracle on 34th Street* on television, a large dinner, and afterward a birthday celebration for Phil. Jane would go to bed as stuffed as the turkey that had been demolished at dinner. She loved Sophia's trifle, which Sophia would only make at Christmas. It was only when she went to Ireland that she learned Sophia's trifle—made with angel food cake from a mix, set to dry for a day and then soaked in rum or sherry, topped with raspberry Jello and placed on the back steps to set in Muddy Water winter, then topped, on Christmas day, with a can of fruit cocktail, whipping cream and maraschino cherries—was as much of a sacrilege of trifle as their family celebration was a travesty of a Christian holy day. Trifle, in Ireland, was as serious as the look on Granny's face as she closed the door behind her on her way to mass on Christmas morning.

"I think she minds," Jane said to Sophia.

"You think who minds what?" Sophia answered sleepily. Sleep being one of the great loves of Sophia's life, she had retired back to bed after presents were opened.

"Granny. I think she minds that we didn't go to mass."

"Nonsense. Granny knows I'm no Catholic and she knows your father is Jewish. As much as she'd wish it were different, she knows you're not going to Christmas mass, without any disrespect to her."

"Still, she looked very serious when she left."

"That's just Granny getting prepared to pray. You just go on about your business and leave Granny to hers. Besides, your Uncle Jack never went to mass either."

"Sure he did. He just came in, and he said he wouldn't be going with the others because he already went to early mass."

"That's just a joke, dear. He's just been up at his club, having a drink."

"Really?"

"Sure. The day that man gets up to go to early mass will be the day it snows in Dublin."

It did snow in Dublin, later in their stay. Everyone made much ado about a sprinkling of crystals on the ground that melted by lunchtime. But not before Phil broke his toe kicking a rock that he thought was a soccer ball covered in snow. Phil seemed out of place in Dublin, and it wasn't just that he was a guest in someone else's house, no longer the man in charge. Dublin was a city of secrets and codes, a city of people who pretended to adhere to a strict social order while living a more lively and less rigid social life.

Phil was too direct and unruly to fit in.

Sophia knew the game by heart and by hand.

Opposites attract sometimes.

Sometimes they spark and ignite.

History gets recorded in a variety of ways.

Official and unofficial, written and oral.

What is recognized as history depends on the sources of the material.

Ireland, that is, the Irish Republic, is a Catholic country where divorce is prohibited by the constitution, reaffirmed in a 1983 referendum.

There is no divorce in Ireland.

Sophia's parents separated in the forties.

Her father then lived with another woman.

But there is no divorce in Ireland.

A scary old man, making people unhappy.

History is constantly changing.

It was April when Gene arrived back in Muddy Water. Jane immediately told him about the Abbott and the head nurse's suggestion. On his first visit to the hospital Jane waited outside Phil's room while Gene went in. Ten minutes later he came out smiling and affable.
"He dropped it," Gene said.
"The Abbott? How?"
"I just pestered him with questions until he said he didn't want to talk about it anymore."
The winter of a patriarch turned to spring.
The spring of a scared old man, so much older than his years.

Sophia never did learn to bake a cake without a mix.
"Why bother?" she said. "I've got other things to do."
Things she liked better.
Freedom of choice.
To bake or not to bake.
It was Phil who enjoyed it, and did it.
Baked Alaska, poppy-seed torte with lemon filling, peach pie with cinnamon in the crust.
Out of love for food, sheer enjoyment of eating.
Which lead to his diabetes.
And the heart disease that killed him.
Curb your desires.
Live life to the fullest.
Phil never adhered to the diet he was prescribed after being diagnosed as an adult-onset diabetic. He was quickly on insulin, injecting his thighs daily. Sitting on the bed in his boxer shorts, needle in hand. Into his thigh, just before lunch.
In deference to his illness, Phil stopped putting sugar in his coffee and on fresh grapefruit. He ate pastries and chocolate, cinnamon buns and danishes, ice cream and bananas with sour cream. He ate dessert after dinner every evening, though Sophia, who cooked dinner, never cooked dessert. Not baking became an imperative.
Phil bought pastries weekly, bought chocolate a month in advance of Easter, ice cream by the gallon. Sophia persuaded the children to eat as much of the sweets that Phil brought home as they could. Containment. When they did, Phil hit the roof.
"There was a whole bag of Danish in here this morning."

"You're not supposed to have Danishes."

"I'm the doctor. Who ate them?"

"The kids must have."

"The whole bag?"

"There wasn't that many."

"There was a half-dozen—three lemon, two cherry and one poppyseed."

"I guess they were hungry."

"Goddammit!"

"Where's the chocolate I left in this cupboard?"

"That was ages ago."

"Where the hell is my chocolate?" Doors quietly closing on the bedrooms upstairs.

"If it's not in the cupboard, it must be finished."

"Goddammit!"

Phil stormed to the freezer in the porch that Sophia referred to as the summer kitchen. He returned with a half-gallon of pistachio-nut ice cream. Sophia watched in silence as Phil heaped it into a bowl, put the ice cream away and disappeared upstairs to ingest the poison and fall asleep in front of television.

Phil claimed he slept with one eye open "ever since the war." Often, as he slept in front of television of an evening, Jane and Gene would sneak past him and change the channel to something they wanted to watch.

"I was watching that," Phil would growl, wakened by the change in the sound.

"I thought you were sleeping," Jane said quietly.

"I was watching that." He rolled over.

"What were you watching, then?" Gene countered.

"Oh, gotohell!"

The spinning earth silhouettes the eastern shore, Venus rises. Jane wanders up the road past the beach looking for Colin. She finds him in the bar, shooting pool on the coin-operated table. Arranges for the use of his truck, wanting to pay him. He says only, "Your father didn't charge me when he saved my life," referring to a surgical complication Jane had long forgotten. The next morning she wakes in August cool to find his truck parked behind the cabin, beside the pile of caragana.

Jane brews coffee and warms her hands on the mug, takes out the mail she picked up yesterday at the post office and re-reads it. There is a postcard from Shulamit, in Montreal. A photograph of blue graffiti on a historic wall that reads "It's Different for Girls." Shula has written:

J.C.:
Bored yet? Communing with rocks and trees, EH?
<u>Very Canadian</u>. Started this graffiti series last month.
They sell. Nothing in hock. "Aujourd'hui, grand-maman est
morte." Going over just to make sure they're relieved. Don't
lose me. Ever.

xox Shula

There is also a short letter from Marie. A love letter, almost, but something is held back. Jane realizes that she is the cause of the withholding, because that is what it seems like she is doing, out here alone at the lake somewhere between Susannah Moodie and cracking up. But it doesn't feel that way. It feels like she is moving as fast as she can. Grinding, digging, holding. Wanting and cutting, listening wide open. Echoing off the morning, blowing in the wind, flowing like a river at its source. Floating when necessary.

That is what is missing.

She is not here by choice.

She is here out of necessity.

Because of meteorites and glaciers, bear cubs and beavers, neglect and caring. She is here because there isn't anywhere else, because she wants to move on, free and easy, confident and loving.

Jane reads Marie's letter again. Thinks about whether there is anything she can say to reassure Marie. Anything she has not said already, anything that she has decided since they spoke on the phone.

Something.

Something has shifted. Centred. Not either or. Centre. Easy, so easy. Skin smooth, thighs soft, hold her cheeks in these roughened hands. Easy down. Jane knows, has known, she realizes, for a while. It is not the choice that has delayed her but the difficulty of making room for another connection.

But it is already made. Easy. Like breathing in and breathing out. Gentle breath, weightless, body to skin. Jane can feel Marie even as she sits alone, warming her hands on a cooling mug of coffee. She picks up a pen, an old postcard of the beach, bathers in dated swimsuits. Writes carefully.

Marie:
Thank you. For your letter. For waiting,
for wanting to wait. Feel like I'm almost

144

home, wherever that is. Will let you know
as soon as I do. As soon as home is.
            Love you, J.

Soft cheeks in roughened hands. Jane drains the coffee cup. Puts the
postcard she has written and the mail she has received on the mantel-
piece. Pulls on her gloves and walks out the door to the truck. Opens the
back. Bends to the pile of caragana. Heaves a bunch on her shoulders,
turns and rolls it into the back of the truck.
Cut it back or it will choke other life.
Over and again.
Ashes in the wind.
Cut it back.
Write your own story.
Watch the sun rise and the sun set, the sun set and the sun rise, and see
in both the spinning of the earth.
How we go on spinning and spinning, regardless.

Snip.

V

JUSTICE

True peace is not merely the absence of tension; it is the presence of justice.

DR. MARTIN LUTHER KING, JR.

It is here where sense begins to be made.

NICOLE BROSSARD
From Radical to Integral

A stone is a rock.

Evolution never repeats a pattern.
Social evolution breaks a pattern, becomes the slow alteration of roles
and expectations. Rocks shifting. Holes in the static of history. Evolution
sneaks through, a new pattern slowly emerges. Dominates. Ossifies.

A stone is a rock. Still.
Rock, move gently to and fro, foster a lulling state of security plenty and
hope. Rock a child in a cradle, lull her and soothe her gently to
rock, sway from side to side,
slowly, easily,
then faster stronger swifter harder rock to a roll
rhythm to a heartbeat draining away
rock the baby rock the cradle rock the boat rock the rock.
Roll it and crack it.
Crush it to sand.
Ashes in the water, the sands of time adrift.
A willow in the wind, weeping, keening.
Wise to the tricks of fate, smart as a whiplash of fortune.
The roll of those unlucky dice.

Bend   lift   heave   bend   lift   heave.
Cool air circling, encircling gloved hands as autumn wafts through the
forest. As Jane fills the pick-up again with cuttings. This is the third day
she is loading and unloading, hauling the caragana, too green to burn, off
to the dump.
The steering wheel is stiff. Jane jams the clutch pedal hard to the floor before shifting. The engine heaves, the gears engage, she bounces forward,

scattering small branches behind her.

It feels good to drive the heavy truck, to ride high above the road, to follow the old highway, the highway where Owen raced the rusting British sports car Phil had given him, weaving and turning. Jane liked to sit up back, her hair blowing in the wind, pretending she was somewhere far away, on the mountain roads of Monaco or California. Exotic and beautiful.

Beauty is.

Jane honks the horn as she turns off the highway onto the dirt road leading to the dump. To warn away bears. Garbage dumps are the great Canadian gathering sites for bears. Jane thinks of the annual gathering of polar bears at the Churchill garbage dump up on Hudson Bay. Searching for food. The trains that haul tourists up there, to see polar bears scrounging human refuse. Jane downshifts and rolls to a stop. The truck door slams loudly in the quiet, her work boots crunch on rubble. She opens the gate of the pick-up and climbs high onto the caragana.

Bend   lift   heave.

Going going going, gone. Satisfaction guaranteed. Neglect replaced with caring. Stone with memory. Emotions placed.

Bend   lift   heave. Change. Years gone by unravelled and rewoven, a pattern divined. Divine. In the heavens, this earth. Divine. This cooling air, this emptying truck, that choking cloak sliced open, scattered to the winds. Ashes blowing free.

The truck door slams loudly in the quiet. The engine rumbles, roars. Jane kicks the clutch pedal hard against the floor, shifts into reverse and puts her right foot on the gas, rolls backward along gravel to the highway. Pulls out and switches on the radio, slamming an open palm on the dashboard above it, the way Colin showed her.

A familiar voice singing a familiar tune crackles in the truck.

Joan Baez sings John Lennon's *Imagine*. Jane sings along, roaring down the winding highway, windows open, cool damp wind on her arms, her face, down the big hill past the beach, clutch down, shifting to second, gas, clutch, shift to first, signal, turn, tires crunch gravel, the sweet pines the cabins exactly as they have been since always, up the small hill, curve right, sharp right, straight on out of the present, down the little driveway, quick left for the first rock, quick right for the second. And there it is, history. Clear.

There is Phil, standing by the barbecue, roasting chicken.

"When will the chicken be ready?" Sophia calls from the kitchen.

"It'll be ready when I say so," says Phil. Pouting.

"Asshole," Jane mutters. Slams the truck door. Then laughs. "Phil, you asshole," she calls out, "I love you." But they are gone.

Imagine all those people.

It's a thin line between life and death, where Phil hovered, with the Muddy River rolling callously beneath his hospital room window, the quickness of spring run-off slowing and thickening toward the drying days of summer. Once Gene was home from university, he and Jane brought Phil to the house on rotating visits, a week in the hospital, a week at home. Life had a rhythm, despite Phil's desperation each time they wheeled him slowly down the hospital corridor back to his room. If Phil had neither hope nor security, he did at least have plenty and soothing, though he could often neither imbibe the food of his wealth nor find solace in the caring of his children.

He wanted to live. Still.

And he lived in pain and in apprehension of further pain.

The only escape was denial.

"Phil—Phil." Jane heard Gene's exasperated voice in Phil's bedroom at the end of the hall as she fried the Swan River hash browns Phil had demanded.

"Phil!" Gene's voice wire tight. Jane left the potatoes and hurried to the bedroom.

"How would you like it if I hit you?" Gene was bent over Phil, his large fist in Phil's face. Phil glared. Gene turned and pushed past.

"Did you hit him?" Jane stammered, furious. "How could you hit him, Phil? Jesus Christ—of all people. You always do that. Here he is giving and giving and you just attack him. What is it about kindness that makes you want to attack?"

Phil began to cry.

"I never wanted to be a burden on my kids," he wiped his eyes with the back of his hand, the image of the hand just brandished in his face. "I'm sorry I'm such a burden. I'm sorry I complain so much—about the pain."

Jane took his hand. "I always taught you kids never to show pain."

"Oh, don't worry about that, Phil. I never believed you anyway."

Later, in the kitchen, Jane passed Phil's apology on to Gene.

"I just wish he'd say something like that to me." His anger had muted to frustration.

"But he can't," Jane answered quietly, "you're his son."

Men show strength in front of other men. Weakness only in front of women.

Cardinal rule of a dying man's order.

And the rule made the pain over to Jane as surely as it made the anger over to Gene.

Son to father, there was no need for iron will. No need for never-show-pain. Not when the son had shown kindness.

Father to son, there was no other way.

A man out of time.

The Swan River hash browns, sliced thin and fried in a little oil, burnt to a crisp in the pan.

After the Easter Rising martial law was declared in the not-yet-free state. As the Imperial Army rounded up thousands for Kilmainham and Mountjoy, the word was lie low, as low as possible. Grandfather Eugene, a young man not yet twenty, slipped through the cordons and took his charm on a voyage to the continent they called America. While seas churned with the knowledge that his brothers and his comrades-in-arms were imprisoned, while winds blew the names of court-martialled and executed poets and trade unionists around the world, Eugene dealt and shuffled, smiled and quipped, gambling his way across the ocean. He disembarked in Quebec City, established contact with sympathizers and then let himself be absorbed in the tide flowing to the west. In Muddy Water, he stopped to have a look around, and soon saw the "Help Wanted" sign in the train station. After an easy conversation with the stationmaster, Eugene took up employment in the canteen of the passenger train which ran between Muddy Water and the west. By then he had noted, with interest, that the country was dominated by a different sort of British than those who smothered the Irish. These British in Canada knew, at the same time as they strove to hide it, that it was only by departing England for these inhospitable shores that they had come to be in a position to dominate by virtue of their Britishness. They had to remain in these outposts, where the roads were mud and the people they drafted as house servants spoke Cree or French or German or Polish, in order to be served at all, in order to have the carriages in which they rode through the muddy streets, in order to have someone to wash and scrub for them. Though they hid it, Eugene saw it. He took pleasure in their dissembling as anyone might take pleasure in observing the emperor without clothes. Eugene undertook his own disguise with all the lightness of heart he could muster, as the roll of the dead called in his mind. *Pearse and Connolly and MacDonagh and MacBride* riding on the wind that whipped across the land. He adopted an urbane spirit of adventure and knew it for what it was. The cities, as they called them, were adventure enough for Eugene O'Connell. He took no interest in the land beyond. The endless forests and lakes appeared all the same, a repetition of one unfamiliar scene to the point of familiarity, and beyond that to a tiresome continuity. At least in the towns there was a little come and go, a little toing-and-froing. The deadly stillness of the bush country beyond the narrow strand of the rails could be forgotten, the grassland, where the wind howled the names of Ireland's best, could be silenced.

Life on the train was series of small but pleasant interchanges, while he served coffee and tea in railway cups, a little biscuit on the saucer. Two and six, Eugene would think, as they handed him the unfamiliar coins. And where are you coming from and where are you going? he would wonder, but not ask, the very questions he, himself, avoided. Sometimes a face would seem too familiar, sometimes one image would draw another from memory. Eugene would smile harder and speak a little faster, suppressing the connection. Like the man who brought Roger Casement to mind, memory conjured by a thin, handsome, bearded face; conjured by his towering height and the sincerity in his eyes as he sat writing in a journal. Eugene watching, holding himself back, thinking don't write it down, Sir Roger, it'll only leave evidence. And the evidence will damn you. The wind had brought rumours of the British government's discovery of journals where Roger had detailed his sexual liaisons with men, along with other facts of his life. Rumours of how a whisper campaign had put paid to any attempts to get a reprieve of the death sentence given for his bungled part in the Rising. No plea for mercy could withstand the detailing of Roger's private passions. Knighted for revealing colonial atrocities, he was hung for a boatload of German arms that never arrived. Do what you like, Roger, Eugene thought, but don't write it down.

"Excuse me." Eugene heard a voice to his left, way out to the west, across the ocean, in Canada.

"Ah, yes, ma'am," he smiled, "sure it's a lovely day in a smarting cold place. What may I get for you, then? A cuppa tea, perhaps?" Where are you going, and why, why are you here?

In Edmonton, in early December, as the short days shortened and the long night of winter descended from the north, Eugene stood by the train as passengers embarked, smoking a cigar and chewing on his favourite questions. Who are you? Where are you from and where are you going? And what has brought you to this land of endless trees? His mind questioned the large women with their double skirts and dated hats, the children who scrambled along behind in handmade suits and coats and leather boots soaked with mud and snow that would soon seep through to their hand-knit woollen socks. He didn't notice the stationmaster approaching.

"You O'Connell?"

"O'Connell at his leisure and at your service," Eugene said pleasantly, feigning a graceful bow.

"Telegram." The stationmaster offered a paper.

"A wire?"

"From Dublin. You Irish, O'Connell?"

"Sir, yes, I am." Where are you from where are you going why are you here. "Lovely land, but not much in the way of opportunity for a young man."

"'Spect it's from your people there, then," said the stationmaster. "Hope the news is good," he added, handing the paper to Eugene's calmly outstretched hand. "If it's not from the army, there's a chance of that," he added, walking away.

But it was from the army. Eugene's army of hope.

It read:

> Past wrongs forgiven. Family home for Christmas. Please come. Letter to follow.
>
> Love, Mother.

And Eugene whistled as he slipped the telegram in his pocket and climbed aboard the iron rail that linked the land of endless trees from sea to sea, for his last run of coffee and cakes and pleases and thank yous. The army had called. It was safe to go home. Carefully.

Standing on the platform, watching all and minding no one as the stationmaster delivered Eugene's call-to-arms, was a short, clean-shaven man, born in Vinitza in the Czar's Ukraine, on his way back to Muddy Water, to see what he could turn up there. Zeda Max.

On the long journey Max bought three cups of tea a day from the canteen, and four times was served by the tall Irish fellow with the small moustache, the too-easy smile and the call-to-arms in his pocket. The first time Max said "thank you," the fellow said something in Irish that he said meant "a thousand welcomes." The third time, the fellow slipped an extra biscuit on the saucer, "Courtesy of the management," and winked broadly. "They're a generous lot."

"It's a free country," said Max, "and if a man works he gets paid."

"And if a man stumbles?" said Eugene.

"Nothing but mud," answered Max, and they laughed.

"Eugene O'Connell," said the man behind the counter, offering his hand.

"Max Cammen," said Max, and shook it firmly.

And where are you going and where are you from and why are you here

Both knew better than to ask.

By the time Max asked for his seventh cup of tea it was morning and the train was rolling deadhead into Muddy Water across frozen snow. Freed, now, from its encroaching grasp, Eugene marvelled at the sheet of white.

"This snow," he said to Max, "how long will it last?"

"This one will stay until the next and that one will stay until the next after that," replied Max, "and so on 'til spring."

"Spring. Exactly. When is spring in the land of endless snow, then?"

"April, May. Usually the snow will melt in April, the rivers will thaw then, but the lakes maybe May, more like."

"The Muddy River will freeze?"

"Sure."

"Solid?"

"Solid? What is solid? Solid on the surface, you can skate on it."

"Ice skate?"

"Ice skate."

"And you do?"

"No, not me. Anglos, French, they play a game they call hockey, with sticks and a ball or a rock."

"Field hockey," said Eugene, "we play it ourselves."

"You play?"

"No, not me. I watch. That and the horses and the dogs."

"Dogs?"

"Greyhounds. The races, I mean. I'm a betting man, myself," he said quietly, thinking of the hounds circling, long sleek legs of the greys, the moment when the bet pays, the notes are counted into his hand and folded into his billfold. The mist slowly lifting. *And Connolly and Pearse and MacDonagh and MacBride*

"Never took to it much," said Max, "a hand of poker, maybe, after the *schvitz.*"

"*Schvitz?*"

"Steam bath."

"German?" asked Eugene, dropping his voice to a whisper.

"Jewish," said Max. "You?"

"Irish," said Eugene.

157

And why are you here

"Here's your tea then," said Eugene, "and a good journey to you." His mind drifted on the wind, to the endless trees ahead, to the letter that should be waiting for him in Quebec City, the hand he might deal once he boarded the boat, the name he might use to slip back into the country, the air thick and soft with rain over St. Stephen's Green, the coal fire burning low and steady in the house on Leeson Street. The soft hands of Grace Barry warming on the fire.

"And you," said Max, thinking of how the steam would feel on his skin after days on the train, and how, once warm and clean, he would step into the cold crisp air of Muddy Water and pay a call on his sister and let that chill-hearted bastard she married know he was back.

Strangers on a train.

Economic dependency rode hard on Sophia's spirit. She spoke fondly to Jane of her years in London, of the opera and the theatre. The comfort of sleeping late, the pleasure she took in enjoying life on an income of her own. The pleasure of her independence. Sophia loved being alive.

"Once I heard Beniamino Gigli sing in a small church. I had tried to get tickets to Covent Garden but they were sold out. Then I heard that he'd be singing in a church, singing for the Italian community. I went hours early and waited. It was marvellous," she said dreamily. "Oh, the range of that man's voice. It brought tears to your eyes."

In London, Sophia met Phil, at a largish party given in honour of the daughter of an Irish poet. The poet was fond of Sophia's passions and her carefree pleasure in life, attitudes he wished to engender in his more straight-laced daughter. He took the two young women to lunch on occasion, hoping marriage-and-home-minded Maire would be stirred by Sophia's tales of adventure in London. To no avail.

Nevertheless, Maire's twenty-first birthday was celebrated in a style which her father and Sophia appreciated and with which she had no affinity. Maire would have preferred a small dinner party with family to the open-ended afternoon-to-all-hours party her father arranged. A room filled with writers and actors, expatriates and patriots from the breadth of the empire on which the sun had recently set. Phil, or "Dr. Cammen, the Canadian," as he was introduced, arrived in the company of Christopher Craig, an Australian cousin of Maire's who had recently taken first to Phil's second in the Royal College of Surgeon's examinations in orthopaedics. Besting Phil earned the young doctor Phil's respect and fostered a friendship of the moment. Christopher Craig had invited

Phil, knowing his uncle's parties to be boisterous affairs to which all who could claim a connection, however weak, were welcome, as long as they were able to converse with passion and spirit. Phil was deep in a discussion of Canadian nationalism with Dr. Craig when Sophia wandered by, a glass of wine in hand.

"Since the war we have acted like a nation," said Phil. "I'm Canadian, that's my nationality. Over here they still think we're a colony."

"It's their habit of mind," interjected Sophia, enjoying the attention of his bemused blue eyes. "For all that I love London and Londoners, the British still see the rest of the world as a series of children in various states of development. It's so condescending."

"It's bloody outrageous," said Phil, who had not noticed British expressions creeping into his speech. "Canada is an independent nation, we're not dependent on Britain for anything."

"You still have the queen," said Chris Craig, "as do we."

"Then it's time to declare a republic. Maybe that'll show 'em a thing or two," Phil declared.

"To the Republic of Canada," Sophia pronounced the toast from her republican socialist noblesse oblige heart, and raised her glass in tribute. Phil thrilled to the smooth roll of her voice and noticed, for the first time, the depth behind the laughter in her eyes.

"The Republic of Canada," answered the two young doctors, who raised glasses and sipped, one amused and the other, enamoured.

The party stayed lively and the guests stayed late, but only a few stayed later than Phil Cammen, who, when he was not chatting with her, watched Sophia O'Connell carefully, to see if her affections were elsewhere engaged. He saw her argue and laugh and cajole, heard her thoughts on poetry, on politics and on the relative merits of Shaw and Synge and Yeats. By the end of the evening, Phil had determined that she had a mind to match his own and wit to go with it, the finest eyes he had seen on either side of the ocean and no particular attachment to Catholicism. He had assessed his own Jewishness, and found, once again, that though he was in and of the Jewish people and culture, he had no particular affinity for religion. Finding no obstacle through his solitary divinations, he set himself on a course toward marriage across oceans.

Sophia was aware that the Canadian doctor's eyes stayed on her throughout the evening, and in her father's way, had surreptitiously gathered what information she could from sources present, primarily Chris Craig. She knew he was Jewish and Canadian and bright. She could see he was tall and pale and handsome, with a shock of brown-black hair, and could not, even with effort, conceal his emotions. But for all that she had seen and heard, it was the passion in his voice that drew her interest and the keenness of his intellect that held her fascination.

It was a meeting that sparked their spirits, though neither would have ever thought of it as spiritual.

From that night in 1951, on Maire Flaherty's twenty-first birthday, when they exchanged addresses and shook hands goodnight, it was only a matter of evenings at the theatre and late dinners in the West End, of silk stockings and fresh fruit obtained beyond legal means, of exploring agnosticism, socialism, nationalism and the role of women in the world, in pubs and over dinner, of wandering through Spain and Germany and France as Phil gave physical examinations to prospective immigrants to Canada and as Sophia, in horror at the surrounding destruction, began a life-long commitment to pacifism, before they stood in a registry office in London, Sophia and Phil both in navy blue suits, and were married.

Across oceans.

Phil had not once lost his temper in her presence. There was no hint of the impetuous fury that he could become. Not until eight months later, with a flat tire on a rainy night in the Welsh countryside, when a string of expletives ripped through the bond of Sophia's passionate marriage. She was four months pregnant.

"I was mortified," she said.

And yet to cross an ocean.

Late August, autumn nestling in the forest. Leaves yellowing, water cooling night by night.

Jane moves to the front of the cabin, between cabin and lake, to re-cut where she cleared when she first arrived. To keep it low as frost sets in, keep it low so that next year she will begin where she has left off, and not at the beginning of time.

Sun warm, air cooling. August quiet. Crouch low, snip, snip, snip, snip. Moss soft, comfortable. Something moving, running, low through the undergrowth. To the shelf, the old shelf standing by the pine, leaning haphazardly where Sophia left it so many years ago. Where Sophia left bread for the chipmunks. Climbing, a chipmunk, up the shelf. Sits, chatters. Jane sees Sophia inside the cabin, staring out through the screen. Stiff. Jane flinches, Sophia smiles, "There you go. Have some bread. Isn't she beautiful?" Jane flinches again, then turns and looks behind herself. Small children standing, watching the chipmunk. A boy, a girl, a boy. They sneak around the side of the house, and a few moments later they come out through the front door. The larger boy is carrying a plastic bag with half a loaf of bread in it. Owen. As they come down the stairs and approach the feeder the chipmunk backs away and watches. They crumble fresh bread onto the feeder, then stand inside the screen door looking out. The chipmunk reapproaches. Climbs, chattering happily.

Jane is sitting, crying on a rock. The chipmunk chatters happily. Jane cries and waits. Thinks of Gene. Maybe this is long enough for now. Thinks of Marie. Comfort and warmth. Almost, almost present tense. Yellow leaf swirling down to the ground. A blanket of leaves to warm the ground before snowfall. Tuck it in. Snowfall. Jane shivers, walks past the chipmunk, up the steps, into the cabin. Sniffling like a broken-hearted child. Turns on the radio as she looks for stale bread. Every barrier crossed opens new ground.

The radio warms, speaks, " . . . lawyer for the Police Association said that the officer is seriously disturbed and is undergoing psychiatric examination. He is under heavy sedation and may be unable to appear before the Inquiry." It is about the investigation into the death of Mr. J. J. Harper, employee of the Island Lake Tribal Council. The officer, from whose revolver the bullet was fired which caused the wound that killed Mr. Harper on a dark March night that showed no sign of impending spring, is the one being discussed in the radio report. The officer, who had been wearing the revolver from which the bullet was fired which entered the body of J. J. Harper on a moonless night in an alleyway, has told his story before, a story that says Mr. Harper struggled with him and in the struggle the revolver went off and fired the bullet which entered the body of J. J. Harper and caused his death.

Certain facts, contradictory facts, Jane the detective now has at hand, due to the dogged quest of the Inquiry justices for information. As she listens, she mulls them over, crumbling bread into a metal pie pan. The notebooks of certain officers on the Muddy Water police force have been falsified. Rewritten. So says the United States Secret Service, corroborating the earlier testimony of a member of the Muddy Water Police Department, who had conducted an investigation of Mr. Harper's death and who admitted to rewriting his notebook. The notebooks were examined by the United States Secret Service at the request of the Inquiry justices, who obtained them after winning a court action against the Muddy Water Police Association, who insisted that the notebooks must be kept private to protect the names of police informers. 1:1, justice versus injustice, Jane thinks.

According to Jane's research in isolation, no witness, outside of the members of the Muddy Water Police Department, has testified that Mr. Harper ever took hold of the revolver that killed him. Other witnesses have said that Mr. Harper did refuse to identify himself to the police officer who was investigating the theft of a car and he did knock the constable to the ground when the constable accosted him while he was walking in the laneway. But he did not, so goes the testimony of non-police, grasp the constable's revolver, the revolver that killed him.

The pie pan is full. Jane stops crumbling the bread and carries the pan out to the shelf where the chipmunk was sitting. The screen door slams behind her. Facts. She puts the tray down, oblivious to the whereabouts of the chipmunk, turns to go in. The screen door slams behind her. Evidence. A good detective reviews the evidence. Jane paces.

A man in an alleyway, was killed by a gun.

The man was walking.

Kept walking.

The cop was talking.

Kept talking.

The cop grabbed the man.

The man pushed the cop away.

The cop stumbled to the ground.

The revolver shot.

The man, in the alleyway, was dead. Killed by a gun.

No sign

of impending spring dark moonless night and a

single shot

shot in the dark.

Separate the cop and the gun.

Immediately.

The combination causes death.

In the thirty-six hours following the event that was the end of the life of Mr. J. J. Harper, employee of the Island Lake Tribal Council, the Muddy Water Police Department investigated and resolved that the murdered man caused the revolver to fire the bullet which entered his body and killed him.

The revolver was not dusted for fingerprints.

It was thoroughly handled.

All this has been public information. In part, it prompted the Inquiry.

On the radio now is the mayor of Muddy Water, a white man long resident in the neighbourhood of the Citizens' Committee of One Thousand. "The public," he says, "is weary of the Inquiry. The issue, which was to examine how the justice system treats the Indigenous people of the province, has almost been lost," he declares. "The Inquiry should be discontinued."

"The issue," Jane answers, to rocks and trees and water and ghosts, "has almost been found."

The gavel is raised.

But, can it crack the rock of foundation?

Foundation, the groundwork on which a structure rests. Shoring it up.

A nation built by Europeans.

On a foundation of people who weren't there.

Trapping, hunting, canoeing, gathering, teaching, learning, trading, governing, sewing, carving, creating. Invisible.

Just like Sir Edmund Hillary, first European to climb Mt. Everest. With Tenzing Norgay, Asian.

Invisible history.

And one lone Inquiry, trying to set it to rights.

The hard rock of the lying foundation.

Crack it with a gavel.

Roll back the rock.

History is collective memory.

Evolution never repeats a pattern.

Change your mind.

Suspect your nervous system of justice.

The little house that Phil bought and Jane lived in had a spectacular garden. Perennials.

As summer broke out of spring, daffodils and crocuses gave way to tiger lilies, irises and red poppies. Jane cut fresh flowers every few days and filled vases with arrangements, surprised at her own pleasure in the task. Each blooming in the garden was an unfolding of secrets within.

"That's a beautiful bouquet," Aunt Ruth commented as Jane arranged the flowers in a vase Sophia had bought many years before. "Baba always said Zeda used to do that, your Baba and Zeda, I mean, my in-laws. He cut fresh flowers from his garden every day."

"On Mackvie Street?" Jane asked, meaning their first house, in the north end.

"Not on Major," Ruth replied, referring to the house in the south end where they lived after he became an invalid. "You don't remember him, do you? Do you remember that house?"

Jane closed her eyes. "I remember that you go in, and there's a living room, and behind that, on the right, is the kitchen."

"That's right, I was married in that living room."

"And behind that is Baba's room, no Baba's room is on the other side and at the back is Zeda's room and we don't ever, ever go in there." Jane opened her eyes, startled at the childlike quality her voice had taken on as she finished retrieving the memory.

Aunt Ruth looked at her across years of silence.

"I never knew if I met Zeda, before now," Jane said slowly, feeling a thick curtain in her mind slowly fade to gauze. "I thought I must have, but I couldn't remember."

"You were very young when he died," Ruth said, rising. "I'll just go have a peak at your father, see if he's awake, now."

She left Jane staring into the flowers, seeing a backyard, a man in a wheelchair with children playing around him. Toddlers. The wheelchair began to sway. Owen—was it Owen?—ran over and scooped a baby in diapers out of the way as the chair careened over and crashed to the ground where the baby had been sitting. Jane heard herself mumbling, "Baby Gene, baby Gene ok now?" Heard the man in the wheelchair, the scary old man, shrieking and groaning on the ground. Parents coming, rushing into the scene as she watched, an old home movie running before her eyes. "Mommy mommy mommy." A young Sophia picked Gene up, took Jane by the hand. "Phil—we are leaving," she said, and walked to the gate with the children. "Daddy," Jane mumbled. But Daddy was standing over the man on the ground, lifting the man off the ground and putting him back in the righted chair. Safe. Mommy opened the gate. "Owen, come." But Owen was standing there, watching his father. Jane watched as the pretty mother took the two children to the car, where they waited. Then they were driving home, with the parents arguing over whether to visit the old man anymore.

"He scares them," said Sophia.

"He's my father," said Phil.

The memory began to fade. Jane noticed the tight grip of her hand on the vase.

Over the next weeks, as Phil sweated and slept, ate and was nauseous, was home and was in hospital, Jane continued to remember her Zeda and his illness. Without relying on or doubting the memories she wrote them out long-hand. A flood of short, vivid film-strip memories in large print filled the little sketch book.

"I'm remembering things," Jane told Shulamit down the line to the apartment on College Street.

"What kinds of things?"

"Things that happened when I was three, or even younger."

"Great."

"It's weird and compelling all at the same time."

"Well, just remember, for now. You can understand it later."

"Don't think just do."

"What's that?"

"Family motto. Phil used to say it when he was pissed off because we hadn't followed his instructions. Don't think, just do. He'd say it to Sophia."

"And then what?"

"All hell would break loose."

"How's Phil?"

"The same, only more so. He's calling, I should go. How's Toronto?"

"Never mind. Go."

"Shul—thanks."

"Drooler."

Suddenly, Sophia died suddenly.

Bob phoned out of the blue.

From far away he said she had felt ill, so he had taken her to a hospital. She seemed better, was talking with a nurse about Canada, then, in mid-sentence, she lapsed into a coma. Saturday night. Seven o'clock. Far away. Thousands of miles.

Jane standing at the window of her apartment. The world drifting away.

Deep sharp chasm along a clearly marked fault line.

Jane called back at six a.m. Chatted with Bob. Thousands of miles away.

Twenty minutes later he called again. To say she had died.

On the Isle of Wight.

I will arise and go now and go to Innisfree

Where she and Bob had gone for a short vacation.

Into the blue horizon.

It was four years after Phil had died.

And only two years after Sophia had stopped fearing him and begun to live happily ever after.

Two short years.

Jane would swear on a stack of any book she believed in that Phil had never hit Sophia.

But she knows that sometime, a long sometime ago, the surgeon's surgeon's hands wrapped around that gentle throat and broke the bonds of marriage.

Hands that saved.

Hands that broke.

She knows, because, as she cleared the caragana away, as she dug up the rocks and examined the precious stones they contain, she found a stone that is Sophia telling her that. The argument, the bitterness, the rough cotton of the flowered bedspread on their bed.

And Jane trusts memory. And Jane trusts Sophia.

And Jane trusts Sophia's memory.

Honour thy father and thy mother.

And thy mother.

Echoes somewhere.

As Phil echoed Max, dying.

In a philosophy of emotion, it is necessary to know not only what happened, but also how the persons involved felt about it, in order to arrive at an understanding.

Human life cannot be understood without a conceptualization of emotion.

Because, as everyone knows, without emotion, we are not *human*.

One   two   three

Scissors

On Father's Day, in the last year of his life, Phil Cammen was at home with his younger children. Jane fried and boiled, sliced and sautéed, laying dishes on the table while Phil sat on the couch watching television. A hot Sunday in June.

"I'm slipping," he yelled, as she placed a mushroom omelette over the faded stain on the old lace tablecloth that Sophia had bought for a song at an auction.

"Gene, can you get Phil?" Jane called. "I have to get the hash browns before they burn again."

"Ok, ok," he answered from upstairs.

"I'm slipping," Phil repeated. He couldn't keep himself positioned on the couch, he would sink slowly into it, then gradually his thin rear would creep toward the edge. But he liked to sit there, hoping the television would lull him to sleep, like in the old days, when he was strong and tense and worked to exhaustion.

"I'm coming, Phil, just hold on," Gene called as he came down the stairs. Then his large hands slid under the sagging thighs and he eased his father back from the edge.

"What are you watching?" Gene asked, turning to look at the television. "*Wok with Yan*? When did you start watching cooking shows, Phil?" Gene picked up the remote control and flipped through the channels— wrestling, a war movie, the roller derby, a football game.

"At least no one gets hurt on a cooking show," said Phil.

"I take your point."

"Get me a bowl."

"You feel sick?"

"I think I'm going to throw up. Get me a bowl."

"Ok, ok."

And Phil sat, as he often did, with a metal mixing bowl that came with a long-defunct electric mixer on his lap, waiting to vomit, as Jane finished setting the table for Father's Day lunch.

Phil dozed as the food cooled.

"Phil, Phil, come for lunch," she said, gently waking him, shifting the bowl from under his arm.

"I'm sick. Take me to bed." Jane felt suddenly flushed and exhausted, the exhaustion that comes when a person's best efforts for someone else have been misplaced. A whole year suddenly threatened to topple. She took the bowl to the kitchen and asked Gene to talk to Phil.

"Father's Day?" Phil looked startled when Gene explained. "You mean this is in my honour? Get me the wheelchair," he said plainly in his weakened voice.

"Come on, Jane," Gene stage-whispered down the hall as he went to the bedroom for Phil's wheelchair.

Phil sat at the end of the table that once upon a time had always been re- served for Sophia, tiny and frail in his wheelchair, with a determination in the face that now seemed too large for his body. Duty. Honour. Loy- alty. Phil's vocabulary.

He did little with the small plate of food Jane served him, but sat quietly as Gene and Jane ate and mopped the sweat from their faces with tat- tered cloth napkins.

"What I'd like," Phil said suddenly, "is to hear that poem about Sam McGee."

"*The Cremation of Sam McGee*," said Jane.

"That's the one."

"There are strange things done in the midnight sun by the men who moil for gold," she began, looking at Gene, who shrugged. "And the Arctic trails have their secret tales that could make your blood run cold." She faltered.

"And the Northern Lights have seen queer sights," Gene continued, "but the queerest they ever did see, was that night on the marge of Lake LaBarge I cremated Sam McGee." He stopped.

"More," said Phil.

"I'll get the book. It's here somewhere." Gene got up to find it on the shelves he had once again, as in childhood, arranged in alphabetical order.

"Now Sam McGee was from Tennessee," Jane continued haltingly, surprised that the words came to her, "where the cotton blooms and blows. Why he left his home, 'round the pole to roam—uhmm—lord god would only know."

Gene returned, wagging a finger at her deviation, and took up reciting in earnest. "He was always cold, but the land of gold seemed to hold him like a spell; Though he'd often say in his homely way that he'd 'sooner live in hell.' " Gene read on through the verses as the promise was made, Sam McGee died and the wreck was finally found. The fire was laid and the corpse of Sam stuffed in. Then, as the door opened on the grisly sight, Phil lifted his head and joined in, "Please close that door. It's fine in here, but I greatly fear you'll let in the cold and the storm—Since I left Plumtree, down in Tennessee, it's the first time I've been warm." Phil felt the heat of the makeshift crematorium warm his chilled body, for the first time in ten long months.

Then all three slowly repeated the refrain.

"There are strange things done in the midnight sun
By the men who moil for gold;
The Arctic trails have their secret tales
That would make your blood run cold;
The Northern Lights have seen queer sights,
But the queerest they ever did see
Was that night on the marge of Lake LaBarge
I cremated Sam McGee."

"Thank you kids," said Phil. "Now if you'll put me back to bed, I think I'll sleep."

Sophia was cremated overseas. Her ashes arrived in a small box which Bob kept with him for a few months, before spilling them on the pebbled beach by their house and setting them to drift in the rising tide of the Atlantic.

And I shall have some peace there, for peace comes dropping slow

Labour Day was always the last weekend at the cabin, before school started. The water would be wild and rough, waves that tossed Jane around when she swam, waves that fought against her determined arms and agile body. Labour Day has passed, it is solidly September, the burgeoning quiet that follows summer vacation. No motors running in the background, a single car parked at another cabin on the road.

The animals come in closer, once the human crowd is gone. The chipmunk is a regular visitor; Jane keeps the feeder well-supplied with bread. There is a brown rabbit that lurks behind the woodshed. Jane is cutting slowly now, but with great satisfaction. It is cold enough that every bush cut low will have to begin from roots in spring. There is something of the future here, of possibility. Change.

Clippers close to the ground, close to the root, close to the bone. Small piles gathered, carried up around the side of the cabin. Rounding the cabin. A deer. Stock still quiet. Beauty in the eye of. Mother. Spotted fawn behind. Silent. Grazes on drying grass. Slowly across the back of the yard, into the bush, hind legs lifting, white tail disappearing. Good company. Company, soon. The closing has begun, the tentative approach to the busy world out there. Almost. Marie. Almost.

In the cabin the radio hums as she switches it on, puts on a bathing suit and an old sweater Phil bought in one of his Boxing Day binges. Phil was always a bulk shopper. Food, clothing, he even contemplated buying a pair of used cars once. During the short period in which he was healthy and alone, food rotted in his refrigerator. He still shopped for five. Jane remembers his suits, that he wore 'til they were threadbare and "shiny," a complaint of Sophia's that Jane could perceive but not understand. And how he would suddenly go out and buy four or five new ones after six or more years of not thinking about their existence. Wear these new ones until they, too, were threadbare. How once she had caught him pretending he hadn't had his hair cut twice in the same day. He came home at lunch, with his wavy hair shorn at the sides and back. And then again at dinner, with it cropped close on top and his neck entirely exposed, reminiscent of his old army photos.

"Did you get your hair cut again?" she asked, without thinking, as Phil sat reading the evening newspaper.

He reddened.

"So what if I did," he snarled, pulling the paper closer.

"You forgot, didn't you? You went to the barber's twice." Jane laughed and laughed, and for once, Phil was silent.

Don't think, just do.

" . . . died by his own hand this morning."

Jane hears the radio mutter and scurries from the bedroom to adjust the volume. "The inspector was chief investigating officer in the investigation that cleared a Muddy Water police constable of any wrongdoing in the death of Indian leader J. J. Harper. He was to appear at the Aboriginal Justice Inquiry today. A letter, written by the inspector before he shot himself with his service revolver three hours before he was scheduled to testify, is in the possession of the Muddy Water Police Department." Jane shivers.

Mystery plain as the act.

Cannot be solved. Wraps a towel around her legs. Stunned.

He will not testify. His testimony is this act, whereby he forfeits his own life and seals his lips.

Tragedy. Always the wrong choice.

Chooses to part with life, family, love, the stars, the moon, his companions and colleagues, his hobbies and pastimes, his very self, rather than explain his actions in the investigation of the death of a man caused by a bullet fired from a police revolver in a dark back lane of Muddy Water on a night when a car was stolen and the Muddy Water Police Department wanted to catch a thief. A night when the moon would not shine and spring would hide deep in the cold heart of winter.

Always the wrong choice.

The gavel, suspended above the rock.

The screen door slams behind Jane. She hurries to the water, picks her way carefully out to the end of the dock, lays down her towel and slips off Phil's sweater.

Toes curl. Legs bend and spring. Fly, glide, dive. Fingers hands arms body sting and shiver. Breath short. Shallow. Roll and float, face warm in the cool air. Arms over arms over legs flutter, eyes watch the sky. Look up, all there is. Sky. Breath runs deep, body loosens. All there is, sky.

A man dead by his own hand.

Jane swims quickly back to the dock, muscles seizing. Climbs the collapsing ladder carefully, pulls off her suit, wraps the towel around, picks up the sweater and scurries back along the dock, careful of her footing on the rotting boards.

Dock, rock, rock, sand, grass, root, root, rock, root, leaves, step.

In the cabin she puts a kettle on to boil, hurriedly lights a fire. Goes into the bedroom for more clothes, shaking with the cold. The radio is still on. Two women are laughing. One of them must be an interviewer. Jane slips into thick sweatpants and a t-shirt, Phil's sweater overtop. Picks up a pair of socks. "Ok," one of the women says, as Jane squats by the hearth, "I'll read, then." Pauses. *"Winter Count,"* she says in what Jane hears as a broad American accent, and pauses. Rolling socks over her feet. Poking at the fire. *"By their own report america has killed   forty million of us in the last century   The names of those who murdered us are remembered   in towns, islands, bays, rivers, mountains, prairies, forests our own names   We have died as children, as old men & women without defenses   We have been raped, mutilated, we have been starved   experimented on, we have been given gifts that kill   we've been imprisoned, we've been fed the poison of alcohol   until our children are born deformed   We have been killed on purpose, by accident, in drunken rage   As I speak each breath   another Indian is dying"* The kettle whistles in the kitchen, drowning out the radio. Jane rushes to the stove and lifts it. *"Never forget,"* the woman on the radio whispers, *"america is our hitler."* And stops. There is silence in the cabin. Jane is shaking. The other woman says, "I think we'll cut to some music here. This is a local band with *Winter Song . . .* "

Jane is standing at the stove, holding the kettle in the air. She puts it down and fetches a tea bag. Draws a deep breath as music begins. A man with a very low voice sings. Then a woman with a haunting harmony. Something about a lake and blood and a breeze. She pours the water over the tea bag, adds milk. About remembering, they are singing about remembering.

Jane settles in front of the fireplace, sipping her tea.

The fire burns, wood she has cut with her own axe.

For years after Sophia's sudden death, Jane would dream-search for her mother. At first, each time Jane found Sophia she would disappear. Later, she would appear, but not speak. Jane would wake with a sense that she was being punished by Sophia, for her wrongs. Unnamed.

Sophia left Dublin.

Left Muddy Water.

Left life.

Left Jane behind.

With memories and rocks, with wishing rhymes and moral imperatives, with the laughter of good years and the longing of hard ones. With a mind that wanted to have done something differently, so that Sophia would return. A body that ached along a fault line death had cracked.

Through the following days, Jane readies the cabin for winter and reads the newspapers voraciously. One article claims that a joke is circulating in the "Indian community" in Muddy Water.
Q: How do you kill a cop?
A: Ask him to tell the truth.
Articles quote the chief of police and the city officials stating unequivocally that his death is linked to the Inquiry.
"And so was his life," says Jane, as if Sophia is sitting opposite, reading in tandem. The officials assert that the Inquiry is putting undue pressure on the police department and want it stopped.
Something is shaking way down deep, Jane thinks, eating cream of tomato soup and a grilled cheese sandwich.
Shaking down.
After dinner Jane sits on the steps, looks at the land she has cleared, the rocks of her childhood playing silhouetted in the shadows of the sun, slowly disappearing with the spinning of the earth. She watches a small girl skip from rock to rock, chatting gamely with her younger brother, then racing him for the dock that is in pieces. She sees their father painting an old canoe turquoise, while beyond him their mother and their older brother swim and chat.
The Inquiry must continue, she thinks, as the two young children jump into the shallow water and begin to splash each other gleefully.
The inquiry into the past.
And wonders idly, as Sophia appears on the ladder at the end of the dock, lifts a towel to her long legs and begins to pat them dry, wonders idly about the history of this piece of land she loves, this place she has come to since she was three weeks old, this plot where she can live in past present daylight dreaming and feel whole.
Who lived here before Europeans declared it a park? Before the government began leasing the land to those wealthy enough to afford to build a leisure-time cabin or those stubborn enough to choose a life in this harsh, beautiful wilderness?
In what way is it hers?
More than these memories, that she already has, and will always have.
More than these weeks or months she may come some years in the warmest times, the easiest times, and turn the ache of longing into memory and so begin to ache.
More than that she cannot claim.

This land, like all the rest, has been swindled or stolen or simply impounded, by the conquerors.

Mute.

Indifferent.

Yielding.

And reserves not thirty miles off. Shoal Lake, Northwest Angle, Big Island, Big Grassy. Ojibwa country.

Ojibwa land, this land she loves.

Washed my hands, in the muddy water

I washed my hands, but they wouldn't come clean

The gavel, suspended above the meteorite lake, above the lava rock land that Jane has cleared for love of memory. For love of Sophia and Phil and Owen and Gene and Baba Edith and Zeda Max and Grandfather Eugene and Granny Grace Barry O'Connell. For the feel of the water light and welcoming on her skin, for the privilege of floating beneath clouds sun stars and moon, for the honour of cutting away caragana rashly planted fifty years ago, imported from Europe to tame the poplars and the pines. Dense cloak, that covered all these years.

She thinks of a sign, hand-painted on a railway bridge one hundred yards north of the Trans-Canada highway at the Garden River First Nation, a sign that says, "THIS IS INDIAN LAND."

As this is, too.

And a gavel high above it.

One   two   three

On a heavy Saturday in July, Phil lay on the couch in the living room, quietly sleeping. Jane and Gene sat nearby playing cribbage.

"Fifteen two, fifteen four and the rest don't score."

"Fifteen two four six and six for three of a kind is twelve."

"Ahhh!" Phil's head slammed back. Back arched. Jane saw his heart at the peak of the arch formed by his tiny rib cage.

"Phil! Phil!" Gene was calling. Yelling. Rushing to his side.

Jane ran for the telephone. Nine one one. "Ambulance." Gave the address.

"Please send an ambulance my father is having a heart attack."

"How do you know, dear?"

"He's a post-surgical inpatient at the Holy Martyr hospital and he's home on a visit. He's had bypass surgery and he's having a heart attack. Please   send   an   ambulance."

"Alright, now honey, calm down, they're on the way."

173

"Maybe it wasn't a heart attack," Gene said as they waited, hovering over Phil. Silent. Breathing shallowly. Jane looked at him. Sad and tired. "Yeah," she said with effort, "maybe it wasn't. But maybe it was."

At the hospital, the son and daughter sat in a room off the emergency ward waiting and not waiting. Jane had a sensation of being disconnected from the entire world. The waiting seemed over, something had happened. The thing she was waiting for not to happen.

A doctor came in.

"We've put him on a pacemaker, a temporary one. He's not in a condition where we can do much more. We're moving him to ICU on the eighth floor. You can see him when he's settled there."

"What happened?" Gene asked quietly.

"He's had a massive heart attack," the doctor said calmly, taking a seat. "We'd like you to think about giving us a non-resuscitation order. Talk to the family."

Silence.

"No," Gene blurted.

"Well, that's it, then," Jane said calmly, eyeing the doctor.

"What?" said Gene, looking up.

"Well, if one says . . . "

"Oh, yeah, I guess so," Gene answered dreamily.

A summer weekend. They phoned Owen, but he was away. Phoned Ruth and explained.

Sunday, Jane and Gene sat in a small room on the eighth floor. A narrow window permitted an oblong view of the open city sweltering under a high summer sun. The supervising specialist of the coronary intensive care unit sat facing brother and sister, clicking his pen and furrowing his brow. His mouth drawn taut as he spoke.

"Your father's surgery was not successful." He seemed, to Jane, to be forcing the words toward her. Jane thought of all the months when it would have mattered to her to hear those words, thought of the surgeon wanting to discharge Phil into her care, and Owen believing him. "He hasn't been getting enough oxygen to his brain," he continued, and she thought of the confusion and the delusions, of the smiling Abbott and murderous Big Bertha. "We would like you to give a non-resuscitation order."

Now, he meant.

Gene stared at the floor.

Owen had not been found, knew nothing of what was going on.

Jane looked at the angry doctor. His bald head, his dark-rimmed glasses, his pale skin. His anger made Jane think that he believed Phil ought to be dead.

"What happens if we don't?" she asked.

"If you don't and he has another attack, he will go on a respirator for fourteen days and then he will be disconnected." Jane remembered the group of Hutterite people she had seen gathered around the bed of the man who had died when Phil was first in post-surgical intensive care.

Gene kept looking at the floor.

Jane said quietly, "I don't want him living on machines."

And as the doctor left, Gene neither spoke nor looked up, but Jane felt his big hand slide slowly across her back.

She had let go.

Phil was timeless.

And she, she just was.

Gene went in to see Phil first. Came out.

Jane brushed his hand as she went in.

There Phil lay, in the hospital gown, a shade of blue she had come to loathe, attached to the monitor she no longer bothered to look at. She laced her fingers through his idle, quiet hand. Cool.

And sat.

There was no more waiting.

Phil opened his eyes.

"What are you smiling at?" he growled.

She hadn't realized that she was smiling.

"You opened your eyes," she blurted, hurt, at first, but then not. He knew. And so it didn't matter.

You opened your eyes, and I could see you then, she thought. But he was already gone.

As day dwindled to evening Jane and Gene sat quietly in the garden of the little house, Phil was too much inside it and too much gone for them to be inside. Drinking a bottle of scotch. Friends dropped by and did not understand why they paid them no attention. Why the talk went round and round and nowhere at all. They talked and talked and said nothing. Owen called and they explained everything and he went to the hospital. And they talked and talked and still they said nothing.

And when they were long past insensible, when the earth's spinning was beginning to reveal the sun again, they crawled into the house and went to sleep.

And when the phone rang at Owen's and he hurried to Phil's house to tell them, just after that sun slid up over the horizon, he couldn't get anyone to answer the door, to tell them that Phil had died.

And when he finally broke in and shook Jane awake she mumbled something and went back to sleep.

And when she finally woke at midday, the earth had spun so the sun was high, raining blistering light on Muddy Water and on Jane's aching eyes, she knew the world was alwrong and Gene had to tell her again that Phil was dead.

But she knew already.

The world was alwrong.

Disconnected.

Jane swallowed two aspirins and phoned Sophia.

"He's dead."

"I suppose you want me to feel sorry."

"No. I just wanted to tell you."

"If you want me to come to the funeral, I will."

"No, that's alright."

"You're free now, you know."

"Yeah, I know." Silence. "Look, if there's anything you want, you know, from the old house, let me know and I'll see it gets there, ok?"

"Ok. You'll feel better when you get out of there."

"Yeah. I should go now. Bye, Soph."

"Bye, dear."

Jane went to the toilet and vomited.

Too much waiting for death.

Shula called.

"I should've come and met him," she said.

"Ah—it's ok," answered Jane. "He was so sick all the time anyway, it wasn't like meeting him."

Old friends, school friends, friends of the family, friends of Jane's youth came to the memorial service.

"I meant to call you all year. I'm sorry I didn't."

"It's ok, I wasn't much company anyway."

"I kept meaning to come and see you, and I didn't until now."

"It's ok, I wasn't much for visitors anyway."

Shadow year. Inside the inside. Too close to far away.

In a philosophy of emotion, feelings must be clarified.

Fear of our own death prevents us from associating with those close to death, or those close to people who are dying.

But we will all die, at the end of our lives. That is a fact we learn to live with.

And if we are lucky, we will only know a short time of pain and terror, before we pass to the state of immobility that we see in dead beings, animal or human. That quiet sleeplike state called death, after life leaves us. It is the pain we fear.

But the wise know, it is not death but dying that can hurt you.

Distinctions are essential.

And the aged and the infirm, the oppressed and the victimized know that life can be taken from you in many different ways
in bits and pieces
and in handfuls and chunks
through murders and rapes, assaults and imprisonment
through starvation and poverty, force and trickery
as well as by illness and death.

Granny and Baba Edith met once in their lives, in the sunny living room of the big house with the limestone front and pillars bracing the wide front steps and the fossilized fish on the northern side of the doorway. They came to see the girl who had been born to Sophia, the girl they called Jane because it was simple and clear and sided neither one way nor the other. The two women, Europeans, one born under the rule of the Czar and the other under the yoke of the British, gave each other a quiet nod of each unbowed and tightly bunned head, across the gulf of their differences and the ocean of their similarities, in a comfortable living room on a quiet street in a small city planted tentatively on the flats of the Canadian prairie. And addressed each other in English, the language of the conquerors.

"How do you do?" said Edith.

"Very well, thank you," answered Grace. "It's good to meet you."

To which Edith nodded and smiled.

"Won't you have a seat?" offered Grace, who was staying in the house and took the role of host.

"Thank you," said Edith, as if she had never sat in these chairs before.

Sophia came in, cradling the child.

"I knew this one would be a girl," Edith said proudly.

"The Good Lord will provide," Grace answered, smiling at the child.

"Yes, He will," said Edith, and Grace met her eyes.

Sophia said nothing, leaving them to their agreement as she eased a bottle into Jane's greedy young mouth. The baby nestled calmly and drank well, as the three—designer, teacher and politician—discussed her features and her future and all of the things a young woman could grow through and could become, in these modern times. Then all three ascended the stairs, turned left at the top, and walked along the short hallway to the small pink room in a quiet corner of the house and lay the sleeping child down for her nap. In that little room beside the narrow staircase that led to the kitchen, a staircase originally built for servants that became the children's path, in that little room the girl they planned and dreamed for, the girl whose birth had drawn them together, flourished and grew into the young woman who dreamed her own dreams, who wondered about religion and philosophy and love and hate and kindness and pain, and what the world had been like when they were her age.

After Sophia died, Jane looked for a reason.
In a causal philosophy, there must be a reason.
People don't just disappear.
But they do.
Ashes in the water.
A whisper on the wind.
Keen, willow, keen.
Finally, Jane had a dream in which Sophia spoke to her. A political dream. Love and hate. Hatred. Jane was dreaming that she was being forced to travel to South Africa.
"But I don't want to go there," Jane told Sophia.
"Of course you don't," Sophia answered, "it's filled with hatred."
"Come with me?" Jane asked.
"Alright, but let's be very careful," said Sophia. They travelled in the dream, as people do, arriving without journeying. They moved easily through the people, unnoticed. The people seemed frozen in place. It was inhabited by white-skinned statues.
"This isn't so bad," said Sophia. "No one even notices that we're here."
"No," said Jane, "it's like we're invisible."
"Well, so we are!" said Sophia, exclaiming, like Alice. "So we are."
"No, it's not that, Sophia," Jane realized suddenly, "it's just that we're white."
But Sophia was gone. And Jane still looking, all these years later.

As the heat of summer gave way to the grief of autumn, Jane, Gene and Owen struggled through what Phil had left them. While the burden of the will and the estate fell to Owen, the job of packing and closing the house was left to Jane and Gene. Jane still ran errands when Owen had sorted out exactly what needed doing. One particular day she went to the registrar of births and deaths to obtain a certificate of each for Phil. Jane drove idly down to the river as she waited for the forms to be processed, the little cards typed and sealed in plastic. The Muddy River slumbered north, meandering its thick and lazy way along the Arctic watershed. When she retrieved the certificates, Jane slipped them in an envelope and drove back to the slowly emptying little house. She only looked at them when she got home.

"Hey," she said to Gene, "his name wasn't really Phil. It was Peretz."

"What do you mean?" He took the birth certificate. "Peretz," he read. Smiled.

A long-ago world vanished just yesterday.

A cold fall night, darkness laying down around her, Jane sits on the cabin steps in a jacket, car keys dangling in her hand. It is time to go. Past time. Marie is coming, on her way west. She will arrive in Muddy Water at midnight. Jane has packed her things in the car. The cabin windows are locked. The water system is drained. The power breakers are off. There is bread for the chipmunk. It is time to leave, to drive to Muddy Water and pick up Marie.

Leave.

Breath wrestles night. Hands sweat beads on the key. Cold, fresh cold. Jack frost nipping. Tender bites in the skin. The far shore silhouetted. Earth spinning round and round. Wanting to roll with it, just roll. Can't stop the spinning anyway.

There is a world out there. There is leaving behind to get there, to come back for, every year. Ghosts of love. Voices. Faces. Moments of home, always. Sweetwater, fires burning, mind slow dancing solo through history. Beavers and rabbits. Dance.

Phil and Sophia first saw this place on a night like this, Jane muses, walking to her car with the last of her belongings. A cold fall night, darkness laying down around them, they walked down this path with kerosene lanterns. Yellow light warm in the welcoming night. Laughter above it. The ease of stride in Phil's long legs, his body safely between the thinness of his youth and the girth of his middle years. Sophia slim, her blond hair wound in combs on either side of her face. Handsome together. Her father extends a hand, her mother takes it. They raise their lanterns to the boarded windows. Peer in between the boards. Inside only shadows cast by lantern light. Jane watches. Their faces breathless. Anticipation.

"Just imagine," Sophia says wistfully.

"It'll be fabulous," Phil whispers back.

And as they turn to face each other, to embrace each other, he gently, she willingly, Jane turns too, and leaves them, not wanting to break the spell of their sometime magic.

I hear lake water lapping with low sounds by the shore
While I stand on the roadway, or on the pavement grey
I hear it in the deep heart's core.

She turns and leaves them, slips into her car and begins to drive. She is looking for a home and a job and a community, a place where there is good work to be done and lots of space for dreaming beneath wide open skies. A place where a woman can be, all that a woman can be, in this modern world. When she reaches the Trans-Canada highway, Jane turns right, heading west. West where the stone of the shield gives way to the prairie, where the earth spins more slowly under the low-lying heavens, where a gavel hangs high and waiting to fall. West to Muddy Water, like her mother before her. On her lap is a copy of the real estate section of the newspaper, on the page facing up, the description of a small house is circled, a house in the north end of the city, where Jane has never lived. Her hands toss the steering wheel lightly, her voice hums a love song.

History is no longer Columbus and Brébeuf, brave discovery and cruel burnings. It is Reb Haskell and Reva crossing oceans, Great Uncle Yossl murdered in the street. It is Great-Grandmother Barry slowly riding north, Grandfather Eugene dealing cards on an ocean liner. It is evolution. Helen Betty Osborne and J. J. Harper, the Aboriginal Justice Inquiry and poets on the radio. In motion. For everyone lost, another to take her place.

It is Owen and Gene. Jane and Marie, one way or another. Any way at all.

As shield gives way to the open ache of prairie, Jane drops her foot down harder on the gas pedal. This is her road. These are her hands, looking for another's. The present is waiting, Jane feels a fault line, sharp and clear from her toes to her fingertips. Definition. Who fits where, who wants who and what. There is a river running, echoes of tenderness, months of distance. There will be clothes in a heap on the floor, two women skin to soft, nestled in each other. And between them only this road and this

welcoming sky.
Head to toe.
Sow to heal.
Rocks that roll.
Hands that cut.
One   two   three
Save your own love.

Memory is alive.

Photo: Rachel Epstein

ANN DECTER grew up in a large Irish and Jewish family in Winnipeg, Manitoba and began writing in her early twenties. She published a volume of prose poetry, *Insister*, in 1989 (Ragweed/gynergy) and her work has appeared in several anthologies and numerous periodicals. Ann has been active in feminist publishing for a number of years and is currently co-managing editor at Women's Press in Toronto. She also writes for children.

JANICE WONG is a visual artist born in Prince Albert, Saskatchewan whose work has been widely exhibited in western Canada. She studied fine arts at the Alberta College of Art in Calgary and the University of Saskatchewan in Saskatoon, and has participated in the Emma Lake Workshops in 1989, 1990 and 1991. A recurring theme in her work is "the space between"—an expanse of space that is also an intimate space, a space both solid and ephemeral.

Now living in Vancouver, Janice has begun work on a project with the support of a Canada Council B grant received in 1992.

PRESS GANG PUBLISHERS FEMINIST CO-OPERATIVE is committed to publishing a wide range of writing by women which explores themes of personal and political struggles for equality.

A free listing of our books is available from Press Gang Publishers, 603 Powell Street, Vancouver, B.C. V6A 1H2 Canada

Printed in Canada